# Debt Collector

## VENGEANCE

JON MILLS

DIRECT RESPONSE PUBLISHING

**Published by Direct Response Publishing**



ISBN-13: 978-1522958895
ISBN-10: 1522958894

**Also By Jon Mills**

*Undisclosed*

*Retribution*

*Clandestine*

*10 Books in The Debt Collector Series*

*The Promise*

*True Connection*

## Dedication

For my family.

# 1

## 3 Days Before New Year's Eve

The private jet's engine spun out a deafening roar as three of the Sicilian Mafia, also known as Cosa Nostra, stepped onto the glistening tarmac at Teterboro Airport, New Jersey. The ground was covered in a thin layer of snow. While it had been a warm winter, each of them was dressed expecting the worst. A short distance away, a luxurious black Lincoln Navigator idled.

One of the tinted windows slipped down. Upon seeing their guests approach, two of Leo Carlone's men, wearing leather jackets, stepped out and huddled together. Their breath rose like spirits leaving their bodies.

They spoke quietly with each other going over what

Leo had instructed. Both were sure of themselves but nervous. A lot was riding on this. There had already been one screw up. They couldn't afford another.

In traditional Italian fashion, they greeted the men warmly with a kiss on the cheeks. One of them opened the rear door and the three slipped inside. It wasn't long before they were whisked away to a small Italian restaurant and lounge located on 17th Avenue in Bensonhurst, Brooklyn.

* * *

Leo's Restaurant and Lounge looked modest on the outside. It resembled any one of the small restaurants found in Brooklyn. Inside however it oozed with style, sophistication, and glamour. Dark-colored hardwood floors, exposed stone walls, and a warm fireplace at the center. It wasn't busy that day. A closed sign had been placed on the door. All of the round tables covered in pristine white covers had chairs turned upside down on them—except two in the far corner. Leo Carlone glanced up from where he was at the shrill of a bell. He sat in a booth, alone, off to the left-hand side. Beyond him was a table with four men. He wiped the corner of his mouth and cleansed his palate with a mouthful of pinot wine before rising. Leo had been running the restaurant and lounge for over twenty years. It had been in the family. Most thought it was a cover for criminal activity but it wasn't. Leo genuinely enjoyed running a restaurant. It was upscale. A mix between a restaurant and a coffeehouse. It had been passed down through the family, and he would have passed it down to his son, Freddy, had he still been alive.

The largest, and oldest of the three Sicilian men greeted him with a kiss on both cheeks. He gripped Leo's shoulder tightly before he spoke, "Please accept my condolences for your loss."

"Thank you." Leo nodded before motioning to the table. "Please. Take a seat."

Leo snapped his fingers in the air. "Arthur, get these two gentleman what they want. And for you, Vito?"

"Just coffee. Black."

Vito Nicchi was the boss of the Sicilian Mafia. His right-hand men were Dominick Morello and Anthony Lombardo. Both of them had been with Vito since his rise to power, eight years ago.

Leo continued eating.

"Nice place you have here. Did you sweep it?" Anthony asked.

Leo paused between bites.

"Do I look like a fucking moron?"

"Anthony." Vito turned to him before looking back at Leo. "He didn't mean no disrespect."

Leo continued finishing off his plate of pasta. Truth be told it had become routine to check for bugs. The FBI were never that far behind them. Until Roy Gafino had been murdered, they only had to sweep once a week. That had now turned into a daily activity. Too many of the old-timers had been taken down and incriminated by recordings. After the death of Gafino the New York Mafia were on edge. Business after business had been raided by the FBI. They assumed that another crime family had been responsible for the hit on Gafino. Little did they realize it was the work of one man.

The death of Gafino had caused a domino effect. The New York Mafia was knee-deep in the advanced stages of a billion-dollar cocaine deal with the Sicilian Mafia. It would have been some of the purest smack ever to hit the streets. Stashed in shipments of canned fruit. The cargo was to be shipped from South America to Italy and then a large portion would find its way back to America via different ports, one of which was Maine. Roy Gafino had been at the heartbeat of the whole operation. He controlled what came into which city. He determined what hit the streets. Along with when and how it was distributed. Without him, business had suffered. Shipments were lost and with that large sums of money were owed.

It wasn't long before word got back to Leo with a name on who was last seen leaving the Pig's Ear before the explosion. Jack Winchester.

"Am I to believe your men couldn't stop one man?"

Leo snorted. “My men? Roy and I were friends, but this is on him.”

“We are owed a lot of money.”

“And you will be paid,” Leo replied.

“When?” Vito asked impatiently.

“Once we have established who will be taking the reins.”

“You expect us to wait while you squabble among yourselves for power and position?”

“You don’t understand.”

“I understand very clearly. None of you have the balls to step up.”

“It’s not as simple as that.”

Vito leaned in closer. “Do you know how much money we lost?”

“We both lost.” Leo stared intently at Vito. “Do you forget? He took my son’s life.”

“And? What have you done about it?”

Leo cast his eyes to the floor. A look of dismay, or despondency crept across his face.

"We can't find him," Leo said.

"And so you want our help?"

Leo lifted his eyes and took a deep breath. He neither nodded nor confirmed. He wasn't one for seeking help from others. But the arguments among the crime families in New York had created so much division. No one trusted the other. Some believed Gafino was still alive. That it was all a ploy to determine loyalty. The old-timers wanted to see his charred remains. Get confirmation from his dental records. They had heard of other crime bosses disappearing off the radar only to reappear and reclaim their throne. Stepping into another's shoes wasn't something that was done lightly. It was risky business.

"Tell me more about this man," Vito continued.

* * *

Jack Winchester had been waiting for close to an hour for someone to show. He sat in his truck outside a rundown house three miles outside of Rockland Cove, Maine. He was doing a favor for a friend, well, sort of.

With the winter season in full swing he hadn't expected to experience such a slow slump.

The past few months had been tough. He didn't need much to live. He'd sold his car to cover the cost of his boat and used a portion to buy a banged-up old truck. Nothing fancy. Just four wheels to get him from A to B. The rest of the money he used to cover a few months of docking, electricity, gas, and sanitation fees. Then of course there was winter storage. Not everyone took his or her boat out of the water but his was too small to leave in. And with Rockland Cove being a tourist area, the high cost of living had eaten into what money he did have in the first year. He sighed just thinking about it. It was costing him more to live on the water than it would if he had rented a room. A lack of funds meant he had to consider alternative ways to make money. All of this meant he needed a place to stay over the winter months.

At first Dana Grant had been accommodating, but that soon changed the closer they became. She had so many questions about his life, and there was very little he was willing to answer. The urge to return to the line of work he once knew was overwhelming. When he took on a regular job doing boat tours, he didn't imagine it was going to be easy. Collecting debts had been his life. He was good at it. Even if it had driven him to commit heinous acts.

He flicked the remains of a half-burnt cigarette into the snow and gazed at the hole it made. He'd been in Rockland Cove for over a year. A lot had happened in that time. For the first few months he'd always kept a bag on hand, ready to leave. Jack wasn't scared, but he knew returning to the town where he had killed five members of the mob meant keeping his eyes peeled. It would have been the first place they would look. In that time, Eddie had told him that rumors were circulating about his involvement in the murder of Gafino. Only once did he feel as if they were getting close to locating him. A few of Leo's men had shown up seven months ago. Keith Welling, the owner of the marina who had become a good friend of his, had covered for him. He told them he hadn't seen Jack. His very being here wasn't smart. If it hadn't been for Dana, he would have never returned.

Now things were different. He had struggled to rekindle what they had before. Dana was more cautious, and rightfully so. She wouldn't admit it, but he knew she lived in the fear of others coming. That's why Jack hadn't told her about the one visit they'd had. In his mind, it was routine. They would have been informed about where Freddy and the others were killed. It was the first place to check. Thankfully, very little information had been leaked out through the media on what had brought Vincent, Freddy, and the others to Rockland Cove. There was no mention of Dana Grant so they never checked in on her. And folks in this town had become wary of outsiders asking questions. After the death of the sheriff, everyone had become tight-lipped. They just wanted to forget and move on with their lives. This meant no discussing what had taken place, especially with strangers.

Jack sank back into his seat and closed his eyes. Maybe ten minutes passed before he heard the sound of gravel. He glanced out to see an old red Pontiac muscle car tear into the driveway. Three guys jumped out along with a girl. They had to have been in their twenties. Tweakers.

Keith had casually mentioned over a beer that one of them owed him several months' worth of rent money for a condo he rented out in the town. He'd also got wind that they were using it as a crack house.

Keith Welling was your typical businessman. He ran the marina, was married but had no kids. He invested his money into properties in and around Rockland Cove. By all accounts, he hadn't run into trouble. Only once did he have to get the cops involved to get a squatter booted out. But these guys were different. He knew that someone in the department was allowing it. Every call he'd placed to them had just fallen on deaf ears.

Well, that wasn't exactly the truth. The fact was the cops had been around but they could never find any sign. They were always one step ahead. And no one who knew them was saying anything.

That's when Jack offered to help.

At first Keith laughed and turned down the offer until Pat, one of the local fishermen, had told him about Jack's run-in with the bikers. That had made the local papers. It wasn't something that was forgotten. In many ways it had earned Jack some respect in the town. Besides tourists, it was tough for newcomers to fit in. Local folk were tight. But that one event had given him a little leverage.

Stepping out of his truck as if he was about to go for an afternoon stroll, Jack crossed the road and walked up their short driveway. He wasn't packing any heat. He just didn't expect he would need it. That was one thing he had made a point to leave at the boat just in case police stopped him on his way out to the house where he had tracked the kid who rented the condo. To him this was a simple miscommunication. Keith didn't want them out. He just wanted to get paid and make sure the place wasn't being used for crack.

Jack knocked twice on the dilapidated door. He

heard movement inside.

“Get the door,” a gruff voice yelled out from inside.

“Why don’t you? You lazy bastard.”

Jack stepped back as the door opened, and a small girl stepped out. She couldn’t have been more than seventeen. She had long blonde hair, thick eyeliner, and wore tight blue jeans torn at the knees and a white sweater.

“If you are selling, we are not buying.”

“Not here to sell.”

“Then what do you want?” she asked.

“A word with Danny,” Jack replied.

She looked him up and down as if trying to gauge whether he worked for the cops. She cast a glance over her shoulder and yelled back into the darkness.

“Danny. Get your ass out here.”

“Who is it?”

She turned back.

“Who are you?” she asked.

“Jack.”

She shouted his name. There was a rustle inside and a skinny guy with long dirty blond hair poked his head around the corner. He was dressed as if it was the summer.

"Don't know no Jack. What the fuck do you want?"

He stepped forward, and the girl stepped to one side. He wore what might have resembled a white muscle shirt at one time though now it was stained and looked as if it had become part of his skin. His jeans weren't that much better. Torn, covered in oil stains, and scrunched up over the top of his work boots. Jack spotted small red bruises all over his forearms. They were needle tracks. He was tattooed all over. One tattoo was of a dragon that ran up the side his neck. In the corner of his mouth hung a cigarette.

"Keith sent me. He says you owe him six months' rent on the condo."

"And I told him. He'll get paid when I get the time to get down there."

He turned to go back inside the house.

"Yeah, about that. You see, he has been trying to call your phone, and he's not getting through."

"That's because it's turned off. Listen. You tell him. I'll pay him when I'm ready. Not before."

With that he turned and slammed the door. Jack nodded slowly, breathed in deeply, and then drove his foot hard against the door. The brittle wood groaned on impact. The door burst open, sending wooden shrapnel in every direction. Danny barely had a chance to react before Jack had a hold on the back of his neck.

"Now. The money."

"Shit. man. I'll get it." He shrank back in fear.

"Lead the way."

He kept a firm grip on him as they went deeper into the house. The place was a complete shithole. As they passed by the kitchen, Jack glanced in. Piles of unwashed dishes were stacked high, others remained on the table. The floor looked as if it hadn't seen water in a decade. Trash bags were tied and shoved into a corner.

The smell of piss and marijuana hung heavy in the air. He had only turned his head for a second when he heard a gun cocked by his ear.

The voice spoke slowly. "Let. Him. Go."

It was the girl.

"Yeah, that's what I'm talking about, Rachael," Danny said.

Two other guys came out of the living area and both of them were packing Glocks. One of them had a thick beard. The other looked as if he hadn't slept in a week. His eyes sank back into his face.

It was one of those moments where he kind of wished he'd brought his gun along just for the heck of it. Instead, he would have to deal with it the old-fashioned way. Jack slowly released his grip. The moment Danny was loose he turned and laid into Jack with what he must have thought was a fierce beating. Jack almost felt like laughing. Danny had about as much strength in those arms as a baby bird flapping its wings for the first time. That was the thing with tweakers, they spent so much time jacking up that they forgot to eat. Their muscles were barely able to control their joints.

"Now get on the fucking floor," Danny yelled.

"You want me to do it?" one of the other men said, stepping forward then bouncing back in excitement.

*God, I hate junkies,* Jack thought.

"Not in here, Danny. I don't want to clean up the fucking mess," the girl added.

"Drag him outside then," Danny yelled.

As the two men stepped forward and took a hold, Jack moved so fast, the expression on their faces said it all. He head-butted one of them. He then twisted the gun out of the hand of the one closest to him and pulled him in close by his long beard.

"Now put the fucking guns down," Jack said.

There was a moment where none of them said anything.

"Listen to him," the man pleaded as Jack tightened his grip on him.

None of them knew what to do. They were each

pointing a weapon at Jack. Their arms were jerking up and down. Their eyes wild and out of control.

Jack lifted the gun under the guy's chin.

"I'll blow his *fucking* head off."

"Danny. Do as he says," the guy yelled.

The girl dropped hers, and the others reluctantly followed suit. They weren't made for this. He imagined that in a town this small, the amount of resistance they got to their demands was very little.

"Kick them over."

The skinniest of them stepped forward and slid them across the room with a quick kick.

"That right. Now go get the money," Jack demanded.

Jack kept his gun tightly fixed below the bearded guy's chin while Danny nodded to the skinny guy who reminded Jack of Gollum. The tweaker raced out back and returned with a metal lockbox. Danny opened it and tossed Jack a large wad of notes.

"Okay. See. That wasn't so bad, now was it?"

"I swear you are fucking going to pay for this," Danny said.

"Really? And here I was, going to walk out of here with the money and tell Keith what nice folks you were." He paused. "Now you have until the end of the week to get out of Keith's condo, or I'll be back and you don't want me coming back. You understand?"

They nodded fast. Jack scooped up the guns and tucked them into the small of his back. He pushed the bearded guy to the ground.

"You guys shouldn't be playing with big boy guns. You really could get hurt."

He chuckled to himself as he backed out and returned to his truck. There it was. The thrill again. It was a piece of cake. Nothing like what he encountered in the city. In the city he would have taken out the girl before the others came out, but these were no killers. They were just college drop-outs who thought they were big-time drug dealers.

He slipped into his truck, cast a glance back at the house.

Danny was outside glaring at him. Jack tipped his head before pulling away.

# 2

Dana was in the middle of winter proofing the upstairs windows when she heard the knock at the door. The house was beginning to show its age. The wind coming off the ocean had battered its walls for years. It was to be expected that things would eventually decay, or break. She usually had it all done weeks before the snow hit, but with everything she had been going through with Jason as of late, it had taken a back seat.

"Be right there," she called out.

By the time she had come down, she found the guest had already let himself in.

"Jack?"

"Dana."

He gestured over his shoulder "I hope you don't mind."

"Of course not. What brings you out?"

"Jason. I told him I would take him out to the bowling alley."

"Oh, right. I completely forgot."

It had become routine, Thursday afternoon bowling. Though it had been a while since they had been out together. Not long after the event, it had been a way for the two of them to reconnect. It also wasn't long before Dana and Jack were back to seeing each other again. It started slow. A coffee at Sophie's, then a meal at the house. A few drinks and they found themselves back in each other's arms. That had gone on for months. And maybe it would have remained that way but then the arguments started.

It wasn't anything that Jack had done. It was what he wasn't telling her that bothered her. If they were to have any form of relationship, there could be no secrets. But there were always conversation topics he would steer clear of. Anything related to the Mafia, his work, or lives he had taken. It seemed to trouble him. But it had troubled Dana even more.

How could she trust someone who wouldn't open up to her? She had told him everything about herself. Nothing had been held back. But he was a different case entirely. It was if he couldn't stand to face what he had done. That had only got worse when she heard rumors that he was doing favors for a few people in the town. Helping them to collect on money owed. She had confronted him about it. He'd waved it off as nothing. Changed the subject. But she knew it was more than that. He had promised that his old life was behind him. That who he was in New York, would never be seen here. Then why was he hiding this from her?

That's when she felt it was best if they took a break. She didn't want to cut ties with him, but she needed her space and until he could be honest, it felt right to slow things down.

She knew that troubled him.

He'd left that night and for a month after they never spoke. Even the bowling had fallen by the wayside. Not that he hadn't tried eventually to get back into her good books, but she wouldn't let him in. She left his phone messages unanswered and didn't answer the door when he showed up. As the months went on, she eventually warmed up to him again. It wasn't like she had many prospects in this town. Besides, Jason got on with Jack like a house on fire. In many ways Jack had become the father that Jason really needed. Someone who was attentive, someone who turned up and showed interest when his own father never had. And yet despite all the good, she couldn't overlook this part of his life that he refused to discuss; his life in the Mafia, his line of work.

Still, as much as she tried to keep her distance, when he was around she felt her walls crumble. She wanted to overlook his past, but the thought that it could in some way endanger them again, ate away at her constantly. That Mafia didn't just walk away. What made him think they would now after all that had happened?

After all the lives lost?

"Oh. Jason's out," Dana said.

"Where?" Jack asked.

"I can't be sure. Can I get you a drink?"

He nodded. "Yeah, okay."

She led him into the kitchen where she put a pot of coffee on. Jack wandered around before picking up a magazine off the coffee table. He flipped through it.

"I know I've been out of the loop the last couple of months. With work and all."

"Yeah, I heard you were back to your old tricks again," she replied.

She saw him roll his eyes.

"Look. I didn't come here to fight, Dana."

"No, but you still haven't let go of what you used to do."

"Dana. It's a few favors."

"I thought favors didn't involve money?"

He never replied. He must have thought she was stupid. Word had got about that if you needed anything sorted out, Jack was the man to come and see. Even the police held him in a good light. In the short time he had been in the town of Rockland Cove, crime had gone down. The police had received less calls because so many problems were being handled by Jack.

"A man's got to earn a living, Dana."

"Isn't that why you took the job at the marina?"

"It's winter. You know it slumps."

"Yeah, but you don't see the other guys banging on doors for money."

He tossed down the magazine. "They don't have the same skillset."

"You mean roughing people up?"

He groaned and ran a hand across his stubbled chin.

"I'm not killing anyone."

She let out a laugh. "Oh well then, that makes it all better."

"Dana."

She poured out two cups of coffee. Steam swirled

above the mugs as she brought his over.

"Jack, why don't you just get a job in the shop? You know, repairing boats or heck, even Sophie, I'm sure she could give you something to do for a few months."

He chuckled. "Yeah, maybe I could be a bouncer on her door."

She gave him a slap on the arm.

He took a sip of the hot coffee. "I guess old habits die hard."

"Maybe it's time to quit."

"Unfortunately they don't hold hitman anonymous meetings."

She shook her head, her lip curled up. "What am I going to do with you?"

"I could think of a few things."

Her eyes widened as did her smile. It had been a while since she had been out on a date with him, or jumped in the sack. She could use a release.

"Anyway, what's going on with Jason?" he asked, leaning back in the chair.

"You don't even want to know." She curled her feet up.

"Try me."

The past few months he hadn't been around much. This wasn't just Jack's fault. The death of Jason's father had affected him more than Dana figured it would.

"You know it's strange. Matt was a royal asshole. He never showed Jason the time of day, and yet Jason looked up to him. It really killed him inside when he found out about his father's death. He didn't say it did, but I know. He's been struggling since."

"Why didn't he say something to me?" Jack asked.

"You've not been around."

Her response was like opening Pandora's box. Right then and there he could have got into a blaming match, but he didn't.

She took a sip of her hot coffee, grateful that they didn't start arguing whose fault that was.

"He doesn't get home until after seven most days. I have no idea where he is, or what's going on. He refuses to speak. He wears dark glasses and has dyed his hair."

"Sounds like your typical adolescent behavior," Jack replied.

"No, this is different, Jack. It's like he's trying to hide something."

"You not picking him up from school?"

"He's sixteen, Jack. He doesn't want his mother picking him up. He finds his own way back."

"Does he have a vehicle now?"

"You really have been out of the loop."

He let out an exasperated sigh.

"He's fallen in with a group of kids."

"Who, Luke Evans?"

"No. He doesn't hang around with him anymore. No, they dropped him off the other night. Tore out of here before I got outside. It was a red Pontiac."

Something changed in his expression.

"You know them?"

"Let's say I've had a run-in with them." He took another sip of his drink.

"You think you might know where he is now?"

"Yeah. You want me to go check them out?"

"Jack. No. The last thing I need is to have him thinking I'm spying on him."

"I'll just..."

"No, Jack. I've got to work this out between me and Jason. Find out what's going on."

"Sure."

They sat there for the next twenty minutes having coffee and chatting. Conversation circled around the latest goings on in Rockland Cove. Rumor had it that the new sheriff was investigating a group of bikers that had taken up residence in the town. They were from the same group that Jack had a run-in with. So far he hadn't heard or seen any of them. But then again, he knew how they operated. One or two of them set up shop like crime families. Initially it was an enterprise. Something legit; a mechanic's shop, or restaurant or café. It was all smoke and mirrors. Once it was running, the others would move in. This had only added to the fear and worry that Dana had. Retaliation by the Mafia and bikers had been weighing on her mind. Now Jason. It was all becoming a bit too much.

* * *

It was a little after six when Jack returned to town. He'd dropped off the money he got from Danny with Keith. Keith was ecstatic. For making the collection, not only had he given Jack some money off the cost of storing his boat in the yard over the winter, but also he allowed him to sleep there.

It was the strangest thing ever.

All the boats were wrapped in outside storage covers except his. His was the only one that was being used. Keith had hoisted it up onto a dry rack.

After getting the address of Keith's condo, the one Danny had been renting, Jack took a little trip out there. It was in town, just on the outskirts before you left. A nice place. The condo overlooked a section of the harbor. Keith owned four of them. He usually rented them out to tourists. It was good business in the summer. And for the most part, he had good tenants until Danny came along. Keith was worried he was going to trash it now they had collected. But Jack had reassured him, a guy like that wouldn't touch it. They were all bark and no bite.

Jack parked out the front. The white condo was lit up inside. Its glow cut into the darkness. They must have turned on every light in the place. It had stone foundations, and the rest was made out of clapboard. Approaching the place, Jack noticed the red Pontiac muscle car. Now this was going to be interesting.

He hadn't been here before. But he'd heard the heavy bass noise that frequently came from beyond its walls. It wasn't that far from the marina. And he'd heard a few people in town complaining about it. That was the only time police came out. Music played here at all hours; a continual stream of dance music at a deafening volume. He could literally feel his body vibrating the closer he got to the door.

Outside were two guys. They weren't skinny like the others he'd encountered. These guys looked like they popped steroids for breakfast. When they saw Jack approaching, only one of them got up. They must have figured that it wouldn't take two of them. Jack didn't bother to stop, he slammed the edge of his hand into the guy's throat. The hulking man gripped his over-tanned throat. Coughing and spluttering.

"Oh don't cry, I barely touched you."

Before the other one could unwind his hulk-like frame from one of the Adirondack chairs out front, Jack pulled a gun and aimed it at him. He gestured for him to leave. The guy didn't hesitate. He darted off with all the speed that could be mustered from someone whose thighs were rubbing together because they were so large.

Jack shoved the other one out of his way and continued into the house. His senses were immediately attacked by the aroma of weed and the pounding of techno music. Lying around on the floor were several teens. All of them looked as if they had just shot up. Their eyes were rolled back in their heads. Jack had to literally step over bodies to make his way through to the next room. He scanned the ground looking for Jason.

The walls inside had been sprayed with bright pink neon paint. One of the wooden doors looked as if someone had taken a sledgehammer to it and busted a hole in it. A broken glass window had been patched up with a piece of cardboard. Keith was not going to be pleased. The damage had to have been in the thousands.

The next room wasn't much better. It was if people had been searching for anywhere to get high. Some of them were just smoking from a bong, but the largest group had shot up with needles. Jack was about to enter the adjoining room when a familiar face from earlier that day appeared. The one with the beard caught his eye.

"Oh shit."

"Oh shit, all right. Where is Jason?"

"Who?"

"Sixteen years old. Dark hair. Has an attitude."

"How the fuck should I know?"

Jack grabbed hold of him by the ear. Twisting and yanking hard.

"Ah shit man, do you have to be so heavy-handed?"

"Where's Danny?"

"Through there."

He pointed towards the kitchen. Jack kept a firm grip on the kid while he navigated his way around the mass of drugged-out bodies. This was Thursday. What the hell did the weekend look like? He knew the town had a drug problem. The inflow of drugs hadn't stopped after Matt. They were still making their way in. They always would. How and where? That was anyone's guess.

Once inside the kitchen, Jack found Danny tangled up with some girl. He had her up on the counter while she was running her hands through his hair.

"Danny," his friend said.

Danny turned, and the color drained from his face. He immediately started backing up with his hands raised as if he expected to get a bullet in the head.

"Where is Jason Grant?"

"Upstairs. Upstairs, man. Second door on your right."

Jack nodded and tossed the bearded guy to one side.

"If I find him with a needle in his arm. I'm going to…"

Jack didn't even get a chance to finish what he was saying before Danny and the other fellow had bolted out the back door.

Getting up the stairs was like trying to wade through thick mud. People had passed out in any space they could find. When he reached the top, he located the room and went in. He shook his head. A naked girl was on top of Jason, riding him. She turned. It was the same one from earlier.

Jason looked shocked. "Jack? What the fuck?"

"Put your clothes on."

Jason pushed the girl off him, she cursed him and dashed out but not before Jack grabbed her arm and looked at the needle marks.

"Sort yourself out."

"Fuck you, man," she replied.

Jason was tugging up his jeans.

"What are you doing here?"

"I should ask you the same thing," Jack replied.

'You're not gonna tell my mother about this, are you?" he said as he slipped into his plaid shirt and pulled at his boots.

"That depends."

Jack grabbed him and pushed up his shirt sleeve.

"What the fuck are you doing?" Jason asked.

There were no marks.

"You think I'm that stupid?" he continued.

Jack then reached for Jason's jacket and tossed it to him. A large white rock fell out and rolled across the floor.

"Then what are you doing with that?" Jack asked

"It's none of your business," he replied.

Jason scooped it up and pocketed it.

"You selling this shit?"

"Like I said."

Jack grabbed hold of him, took out the rock and

tossed it.

"Get the fuck off. You're not my father."

"You want to end up like your old man?"

"Who cares?"

"Your mother. Me."

"Right. Like you've been around lately."

He stormed out and Jack followed after.

"I've been busy with work."

"Yeah, I heard you showed up at Danny's. What's my mother think about that?"

They trudged their way around stoned teens.

"Don't spin this back on me. Your mother gives a shit about you. You get caught up in all this and you are liable to end up dead."

Jason spun around and came back at Jack.

"You don't get it, do you? These people. Danny and the others, they…"

"Give you a sense of belonging?" Jack cut him off. "I get it. I was drawn to the same shit when I was young. But this isn't the way, kid. These people don't care about you. The moment you stop being of use to them, they will dispose of you. And if they don't, whoever is feeding them this crack, will."

Jason stared intently at him before shaking his head and exiting the condo. Outside he got into Jack's truck. Jack eyed him as he came around to the driver's side. A few minutes later as they made their way back to Rockland Breakwater Lighthouse, Jason broke the silence.

"Why did you show up?"

"Because your mother's worried. She's got enough on her plate without having to deal with this," Jack replied.

"How did you know I was there?"

"Do you really expect me to answer that?"

Jason gazed out the window.

"This ain't you, Jason. What is going on?"

"Nothing."

"Your mother thinks it's about your father."

"It's nothing to do with him. I just need money."

"I can relate to that. But there are other ways of

earning it."

"What, like beating on guys like Danny?"

Jack leaned his head to one side. He had to see the irony in it all.

"You know how much I'm bringing in with this?" he paused. "One grand a week. Tell me. Where can I earn that kind of money?" Jason asked.

Jack shook his head. "That's how they pull you in, Jason. The money. It all looks good until you see a friend with a bullet in his head."

"They don't go looking for trouble," Jason spat back.

Jack swerved the truck over. "Trouble finds you. All it takes is one deal to go wrong and someone to rob you. And it's over."

"That ain't gonna happen."

Jack chuckled at his response.

"Because I've got this," Jason said.

Jason reached into his jacket and pulled out a 9mm. Jack had it off him before he could point it. He slipped out the magazine.

"Where did you get this?" Jack asked.

"Where do you think?"

Jack rolled his window down and tossed out the gun without the mag into a bunch of brambles.

Jason knit his brow together. "What the hell, Jack? That's the only one I've got," he yelled.

"And that's the last one. You are only sixteen."

Jason was about to jump out to retrieve the gun when Jack locked all the doors and pulled away. Again there was silence for the remainder of the journey back to the house. When they pulled up Jason tugged on the door.

"You gonna let me out?"

"Listen, I'm sorry, Jason, about not being around lately or for embarrassing you in front of that girl. But there is a lot of nasty shit going on and I don't want to see you get caught up in it."

"Yeah, well. You won't have to worry about that soon."

"Why?"

"My mother's thinking of moving."

Jack's eyebrows shot up in surprise. "What?"

"Will you let me out?" he asked again.

"Yeah." Jack unlocked the door and Jason jumped out. He strolled over to the house while Jack contemplated what he'd just told him.

# 3

Orderlies dressed in white were going about their duties of helping patients at the East Star Behavioral Treatment Center when Vito's men rolled up in a dark SUV. Vito had sent Dominick Morello and Anthony Lombardo to take care of Jack Winchester while he and Leo Carlone made plans for distributing a new line of narcotics. The DEA were getting better at stopping their shipments. They needed to find shipping areas that weren't known for having loads checked.

Leo was going to send a few of his own men along but Dominick assured him it wouldn't be necessary. This wasn't going to take long and the fewer people who showed up the better. They didn't want to give anyone a reason to call the cops. Not that the cops were an issue. Leo had four of them on the payroll and that even included someone in the FBI. It was the reason they had managed to stay out of jail for so long.

Dominick and Anthony were in their early thirties. They had grown up in the Mafia. Like many others, they didn't choose to get into it; they were a part of it because their fathers held prominent positions. It was the way it was. From father to son, the work was passed down. However, these two didn't excel in areas of business. They were thugs. The ones who got their hands bloody. By all accounts they kept to themselves and only came in when a person had to disappear or pay.

"You buy what Leo said about this guy?"

"He's a man, Anthony, not a machine. I've seen his type before."

"But he killed some of their best."

Dominick stopped walking and turned to him.

"They obviously weren't the best. Now grow some balls."

"Yeah, that's what you said with that guy in Catania. Look how that turned out."

The Sicilian Mafia were set up in cities throughout Italy. They faced the same challenges that their associates did in New York. They had their hands in every kind of racket and criminal activity: sex trafficking, offshore Internet gambling, narcotics, extortion, money laundering, and prostitution. It was all up for grabs.

The Mafia in Catania had suffered their own setbacks when one of them had turned the tables on them and become a rat. The problem was he was the best at what he did — which was killing. Dominick and Anthony had been sent in to find him and end it. What should have been a few days turned into weeks as they found themselves chasing a ghost. He always remained one step ahead of them.

When they eventually caught up with him, they nearly lost their lives in the process. Anthony was stabbed, and Dominick shot. Regardless, they finally brought him down. That's what they were paid to do. Kill. For the past eight years they had lost track of the number of people they had shot, stabbed, decapitated, and buried. The mobster from Catania, however, was one kill they couldn't forget. It had been one of the hardest fights of their lives. The guy was as tough as nails. Anthony hadn't been able to shake the memory of that day. The scar across his face, and the wound in his side served as a constant reminder. Anthony was now cautious whereas Dominick charged ahead into a situation with little thought to how it would end.

"It will be different this time."

They had learned a lot from Catania.

Inside the treatment center, a few of the staff looked over at the men. A look of fear, perhaps worry gripped them. At the front desk a lady punched keys while glaring at her computer screen. She looked as if she hated her job. The years had taken a toll on her. Grey hair was spreading throughout what was once lush black hair. She glanced up at the men.

"Can I help you?"

"We're here to see Milly Winchester."

"You are?"

"Relatives."

Her eyes darted back and forth between them. She spun in her seat and tapped away on another computer.

"What did you say your names were?"

When she turned back, they were gone. Two officers were now in their place. She widened her eyes and cast a glance down the hall.

"Ma'am?"

"Did you just see two men?" she asked.

"No," the officers replied, casting a glance down the corridor.

"Huh," she said.

Dominick had spotted the officers come in. Until they knew which ones were working for Leo, they weren't taking any chances. They had slipped around the corner and ducked into a washroom. With the door cracked they could hear the conversation. Once the coast was clear, they slipped out unnoticed and left. They would return later. Everything they did was precise. They kept out of sight from police. They were mindful of how they spent their time. They left little trace that they had been there. That's why Vito paid them well. Dominick made a note to grab the security footage.

* * *

The next morning Jack was heading out to the lighthouse. He hadn't been able to sleep much that night. He kept mulling over what Jason had said about them moving. Why hadn't Dana said anything? Sure, they had some differences. He knew she wasn't keen on him doing any kind of work that resembled his life before Rockland Cove, but moving without telling him?

Jack rolled out of bed. His body ached. It felt as if he had pulled a muscle. He wasn't getting any younger and now he was starting to feel it, even if he was only thirty-eight.

He tossed yesterday's coffee grounds into the garbage and tossed in a few scoops. As he was putting some toast on, his phone began vibrating on the table. He ambled over. The caller ID read, Eddie Carmine. He tapped accept and left it on speaker while he continued preparing breakfast.

"Eddie. A bit early for you, isn't it?"

He chuckled on the other end. "Eight isn't early. I've been up for four hours."

"That's what a weak bladder will do for you."

He laughed.

"So are you going to make it down?"

"I don't know. Something's come up."

"Jack. C'mon. She's been waiting to see you. It's New Year's Eve. You can't miss this."

"I know. How's she doing?"

"She's doing good. I picked her up this morning."

"How long's she out?"

"Just the weekend," Eddie replied.

He breathed in deeply before bringing the cup to his lips and letting the caffeine kick start his senses.

"I'll get back to you today," Jack said.

"It's Dana, isn't it?"

Jack took another swig.

"Her son. And yeah, Dana."

"Why not bring them down? You know. Give me a chance to meet this woman?"

"Maybe. I'm really not sure where I stand with her right now."

"What do you mean?" Eddie asked.

"Some days are good. Others I'm really not sure."

"What's the issue?"

"My life."

"But you left it all behind for her."

"Sort of."

"Jack?"

"Listen, you got to pay the bills, right?"

"Please tell me you have not gone back to collecting."

"It's not like in New York. These are simple jobs. Just favors really."

"Favors?"

"Yeah. Small issues. No one gets injured."

"Really?"

Jack let out a small laugh.

"You know your problem, Jack, is you need to decide what you are fighting for."

"I wish it was as easy as that."

"Listen, give me a call later. Let me know either way."

"Sure thing."

Once he hung up, he sat down with his coffee and toast and gazed out the window. His view of the harbor was blocked by numerous boats. He thought back to when he was young. Eddie was always trying to teach him lessons. In between showing him how to defend himself, Eddie always came up with these analogies about life that he could never quite figure out.

"There's a lesson in everything, Jack," Eddie had said.

"I don't get it," he had responded.

"Neither do most. They spend their lives living on the surface. Just seeing the obvious. But I want you to look below the surface. Think about why you do things. Think about the situations that you walk into. Think about an exit strategy. You need to look below the surface. See what others don't. There is always something going on. Small things teach us a lot about people. What they are capable of, what they are hiding, what they are planning on doing before they do it. The battle isn't always won by the toughest in the room, but by the smartest. Sometimes you will walk away, other times you must fight."

Jack chuckled to himself over the memory as he continued his breakfast. So many years had gone by. He wouldn't want to relive his youth, but Eddie had been a lifeline in the worst storm of his life. He'd taught him how to survive. How to stay calm in tight situations. To never give up until you took that last breath.

* * *

One hour later, as he rolled around the corner that brought him onto Lighthouse Road, a car shot by; Danny's red Pontiac. It had to have been traveling at over seventy miles an hour. It was going in the opposite direction. Heading towards town.

Another ten minutes and he was killing the engine outside the house. He got out and hustled over to the door. The wind was howling and snow was coming down heavy. It was just after nine in the morning. After he knocked on the door and waited briefly, Dana opened up. She had tears in her eyes. Her face looked red as if she had been crying for a while.

"What's up?"

Jack immediately stepped inside.

"Nothing. I…"

"Dana."

She shook her head. "I had a big argument with Jason this morning. He just blew up in my face."

"About moving?"

"How do you know about that?"

Jack closed the door behind him.

"Come on. I'll make you a coffee," Jack said.

Inside you could hear the sound of the ocean. A few

windows were partly open, letting in a freezing cold breeze.

"You hot or something?" he asked.

He pressed them closed, and it went silent.

"I just needed to get some air."

Jack took down two mugs. He ground up some fresh coffee beans, put them in the coffee maker, and wiped down the counter while he looked at Dana. He had only seen her cry a few times. On each occasion it tore him up. Dana curled up on one of her lounge chairs while he prepared the drinks.

A few minutes passed, he brought her cup in and handed it to her.

"I found a bunch of drug paraphernalia in his closet. Along with some drugs. I don't know what's going on with him but this crowd he's going around with, I'm sure they're responsible. Where did you find him last night?"

Jack took a sip of his drink, wondering if she should tell her. He rubbed the bridge of his nose.

"At a condo in town."

"Where?"

"It doesn't matter."

"Jack," she said.

"Keith rents out condos. Seems the crowd he's running around with are into drugs. Distributing."

"Oh God. I suck at being a mother."

"Listen, it's not your fault. You can't watch him every moment of the day. The kid is growing up and he'll tell you one thing and do another."

"I knew it though. The way he covered up his face. He's using, isn't he? My sixteen-year-old is using drugs."

"I'm not sure about that. I checked his arms."

"His arms!" Her voice rose. She placed a hand over her face as tears streamed down.

"What happened this morning? Why didn't you tell me you were thinking of moving?"

"Because I knew that you would react and I'm just so tired of dealing with confrontations."

"What? Were you just going to take off without

telling me?"

"Jack. We're not together. I'm sure I made that clear."

Jack sighed. "If I was doing something else for a living. Just the boats or something else, would that change your mind?"

"But that's not you, is it?"

"Who's to say that's not me?"

"Jack. I applaud your attempt to try and change things. To try and walk away from who you are. But look at what you're doing now. It's what you do."

Jack groaned.

"That's why I want to get out of this town. There's just too many bad memories. I'm always wondering if someone else is going to show up."

"But..." Jack tried to cut in.

"I know you said that no one will, but that doesn't reassure me. And with all the stuff that Jason is going through, it just seems the right thing to do. We all need a fresh start."

"So where will you go?"

"I don't know. I need to be close to here for my work, but even that. I've told Sophie I might find another job. Start again elsewhere."

"So you've already made up your mind?"

She shook her head. "Yes. No. I don't know what I want."

There was a pause while she caught her breath and wiped away the tears.

"Why don't you come with me to New York?"

"What?"

Jack put his mug down and came over to her.

"New Year's Eve is coming. Eddie phoned and invited me down. It would give you a chance to meet my sister. Think it over."

"I don't know, Jack."

"Look. If this thing between you and me isn't what you want. If you are set on moving away, then okay. But give me one more chance to…" he paused. "Give us one more chance."

She studied his face. It was strange how a year could change things between two people. The honeymoon period soon vanishes. That sense of what is new and untainted soon becomes old. The reality of who you are with dawns on you. He never expected it to be easy. It was probably the reason why no relationship of his had ever lasted. It was easier to sleep with women and move on. But this was meant to be different. He had tried to give it his best shot. And for a short while it had gone well.

When Leo's men had shown up, though, it had confirmed his own fears. The past was not behind him. Walking away from the Mafia wasn't easy. Most entered witness protection or put a bullet in themselves before anyone else did. You cut ties with everyone. But Jack still had ties. Someone who they could use against him. He had considered bringing his sister up to Rockland Cove but that wouldn't have worked either. He had enough on his plate. At least where she was, she could get treatment and Eddie checked in from time to time. He was glad she was getting better. That some smidgen of who she was before the damage was returning. Perhaps, it wouldn't be long before she was ready to come out.

As much as Eddie had convinced him that he needed to come down and see her for himself, he was worried that by seeing her again, that his face alone might trigger repressed memories from their childhood. The beatings that both of them received, the times he couldn't protect his sister from his father, and the trauma of losing their mother.

"Why does everything go to shit?" she asked.

"I'm sorry, Dana. Really," he replied.

He didn't want to be a thorn in her side. She had enough to deal with, with Jason.

"You don't have anything to be sorry for, Jack. It can't be easy trying to walk away from all that you've ever known. And well, I thought I had brought Jason up to know better." She let out a long breath. "If his father had stayed clear of the drugs, maybe this wouldn't have happened."

It was tough walking into someone else's life. Everyone had baggage, history, and people that had affected them.

"Look, I'm going to head out tomorrow morning. If you want to come to New York, give me a call."

She nodded, briefly biting gently down on her lower lip.

* * *

Around one that afternoon, Jack met up with Keith and Carlos in the local bar down at the marina. Keith owned the place. When he walked in, they were already in the thick of conversation over a Celtics game playing on the TV.

"Hey Jack." Keith waved him over.

They had several pitchers of beer and had ordered a variety of chicken wings. The place smelled like fried chicken and peanuts. Staff were circling tables. The clink of cutlery could be heard. A glass smashed in the kitchen.

He took a seat.

"So any word on Danny moving out?" Jack asked.

"I swung by there this morning. Nothing yet. Looks like we are going to have to call the police in," Keith said.

"No. Leave it to me."

"Jack, what did you do before this?" Carlos asked.

He'd always kept quiet. He didn't want to raise any questions or put anyone in a position where they would have to lie. Instead he had told them that Rockland Cove was a new start, a means to escape a life that wasn't good for him. They had simply notched it up to a bad marriage. He'd told Keith if anyone came asking for him to say he wasn't around. At first Keith had badgered him about that but eventually he let it go.

"So? What did you do?" Carlos asked again.

"You don't want to know, I'd have to kill you," Jack replied. The others started laughing.

# 4

When Dominick and Anthony returned to the treatment center that evening, it was quiet. They had a large security guy on site but nothing that they couldn't handle. It was your usual overweight and aging guy, the type who couldn't get into the police so he was forced to take a job working for some shitty security company. Tonight would be his unlucky night.

When they approached the front desk a different person was manning the phones. They asked again to see Milly Winchester.

"Unfortunately, visiting hours are over. You will need to come back in the morning."

Dominick cast a glance at Anthony and smiled.

"That's going to be a problem. You see, we're only in town for a short while."

"Sorry. Nothing I can do, guys."

"Can we speak to your supervisor?"

The woman immediately frowned. A look of disgust crossed her face as she rolled her eyes and let out a sigh. Dominick could tell she wasn't in the mood for anyone's crap tonight. But neither was he. No doubt she had planned on having a quiet evening. She was about to get it. The moment she turned her back, Dominick pulled out a Walther P22 with suppressor and fired a round into her head. The woman dropped like a sack of potatoes. A pool of blood began forming around her hair. As cool as ice, Anthony went around to where she was as Dominick turned his attention on the security guard who had witnessed it and was scrambling to get out of his chair. He'd obviously eaten one too many donuts.

Two more shots and he dropped as well. While Anthony pulled Milly Winchester's file, Dominick went searching for the security room where the recording equipment was kept. It didn't take him long to find it. He entered the small room using a keycard that was on the dead security guy. He was expecting to find another security officer, but it was empty.

When he returned from destroying the equipment, he found Anthony wrestling with an orderly.

"He says she left for the weekend."

"And the address of Jack?"

"They don't have it on file. They just have a number for an answering service."

Dominick watched Anthony choke the guy to death before they left with the number. They left behind them a trail of blood.

* * *

Later that evening Detective Frank Banfield of the New York Police Department sat looking over photos that he'd gone over countless times. A convenience store's surveillance camera located across from the Pig's Ear had caught a vehicle pulling away after the explosion. The photos were grainy at best even with the technology they had used to clean them up. It had been dark that night, and the camera had never got a clear shot of the plate, nor the figure.

He'd been told through the grapevine after coming down heavy on some local crime families that they believed Jack Winchester was responsible for the explosion. He kind of hoped that wasn't the case. His gut told him it was Jack, but logic said that it had to be a rival crime family. They were forever doing these kinds of things. Usually it was fighting over territory. He couldn't wrap his head around why Jack would turn on the hand that fed him.

On the surface most might have assumed it would have been easy to track him down and pull him in for questioning. But the man was a ghost. Frank Banfield had grown up with Jack. They had been friends from the age of nine until Jack fell in with Gafino's men. It was tough to think that they had gone in such opposite directions. He knew Jack had a rough family life. He'd seen the bruises on him at school. But they were from opposite sides of the tracks. They may have never met if Jack hadn't stuck up for him.

At the age of nine he'd been bullied by a group of

kids on the way home from school. They had taken his bag, given him a black eye, and taken turns laying into him. Frank Banfield was from a Jewish background. The boys taunted him about wearing a yarmulke. It was a skullcap that had to be worn while praying, eating, or studying as a sign of respect. Though most of the time he removed his and hid it in his bag to avoid the constant bullying.

Jack didn't have to intervene that day. He could have walked on by and avoided getting a cut lip, but he didn't. They might have been outnumbered but he made them think twice about laying into Frank in the future. That was enough. From then on, they walked home together. Exchanged baseball cards and occasionally hung out when Frank could sneak out. Frank would never forget that. But things were different now. This was murder and no matter what he had done as a kid, he had a job to do.

Over the years, they had passed each other on the streets. There was a mutual respect for each other. Frank knew that Jack had killed people. But he couldn't prove it. Jack was clean. He didn't leave a trace of his involvement in a crime. So catching him on video, or at least the silhouette of someone that could have been him, was a sign of sloppiness. It wasn't the way he usually worked. At least from what Frank had learned. Over his career he had been called out to numerous murder scenes. Most of the bodies had their teeth removed. That was common. The ones that pointed to Jack were the bodies that had been frozen. This was done to obscure the time of death. Though more times than not, the bodies were never found. Word soon spread on the streets. Jack's reputation grew. As did Frank's but for very different reasons. People learned to fear Jack because he showed no mercy. Frank was the same, however he didn't kill them, he just locked them up.

Only once did he ever speak to Jack beyond a head nod or a passing glance. Even then it was barely a conversation. He had found Jack inside St. Patrick's Cathedral one Christmas. Frank's partner at the time was a Catholic. It had become routine to go to the cathedral and light a candle. Many times Frank would wait outside for his partner, but that evening he'd gone in to keep out of the cold. There were very few people there. Ten at the most, in a cathedral that size, meant it looked empty. Near the back he spotted Jack. He wasn't praying. He didn't have his head down. He just sat quietly staring forward.

Frank took a seat beside him.

"Come to arrest me, Frank?"

He chuckled. "Soon, Jack. Not today."

"It's relaxing, isn't it?" He looked around. "This place."

"I never thought you were religious?" Frank asked.

"I'm not. But that doesn't mean I don't think there is something out there that guides our path."

He cast him a sideways glance. "You want to make God responsible for your path, Jack?"

"Do you think he guides you, Frank? To catch criminals?"

"Maybe."

"Why not just stop them before they do it?"

Frank breathed in deeply. "Perhaps he has a strange sense of humor."

Jack snorted. "Maybe."

Jack rose to his feet.

"I'll see you around, Frank."

"Not if I see you first."

"Merry Christmas."

Frank nodded.

He drifted back to the present as a phone call came in. On the other end was another detective.

"Seems we've got a triple homicide down at the East Star Behavioral Treatment Center."

"I'll be right there."

* * *

Eddie Carmine had grown up on the streets of Brooklyn. He'd watched countless kids get caught up in crime. He had been tempted to get involved and for a short while he had run errands until a friend of his was shot. That changed everything. Unlike others who would have overlooked it, continued on, and notched it up to life in the Mafia, he couldn't.

His father had been a blue-collar worker who was involved in construction. He'd learned a lot from his old man. It might not have been as easy as running with the mob, but it was honest. And that mattered to him. By the age of eighteen he had enlisted in the military at the prompting of his father. He knew that his father really didn't want him in it, but the alternative was getting caught up in a life of crime. He was grateful for that decision. It was what made him who he was today.

He learned to live by rules. He put in years of regular service before being asked to be a part of the Marine Corps Special Operations division. They were the elite. Few were asked. Most of his missions were special reconnaissance or direct action.

By the time he came out of the military he was thirty-one. He had gained a skillset that was geared for killing people. However, there were very few jobs that let you do that unless you got involved with the Mafia — which wasn't an option for him.

By that time, Roy Gafino had been making waves in Manhattan. He was younger back then. Roy was an up-and-coming kid who Eddie knew. They had run together. It wasn't strange to think that he ended up becoming a boss in the Mafia. But the truth was you either joined the mob, became a cop, or wound up paying protection money. There were few other options that made sense. Those who knew him in the neighborhood welcomed Eddie back with open arms; Roy Gafino was one of the few who didn't.

Perhaps he thought Eddie had chosen a path that was better than his. Maybe he thought Eddie looked down on him. He was never really sure why they became at odds with one another. They were friends when they were youngsters but then they led very different lives. Roy had tried numerous times to get Eddie to leave his job at the factory. He flashed money, gave extravagant gifts, and told him about the perks of his trade.

But Eddie knew better. He watched as friend after friend either died or wound up serving time. That was the risk. Instead he chose to live beneath the surface. He kept his nose clean, showed up for work on time, and went about leading a quiet life.

He practiced martial arts daily. Ate well, never drove a vehicle, and continued to rise early. It was consistency that the military had drilled into him. That was what made you good at anything. Showing up before you were meant to. Being the last one to leave. Dedication to the mind and body and always being prepared to fight. These were the same attributes and principles that he had tried to instill in Jack.

He knew what people were saying about him. He'd met Jack's mother before he went into the military. They had been with each other. There was a good chance Jack was his. The likeness was similar but not enough that it was clear. By the time he got out of the military she was no longer around. Word had it that she died in childbirth. But he knew that wasn't true. He'd asked around. Spoken to a few people down at the local hospital. They all said she went missing a few weeks after Milly was born. Eddie figured Jack's father had killed her. He was a drunk and was known for beating on her. The hospital had a long record of the number of times she had shown up with black eyes and split lips.

At first, Eddie never enquired if Jack was his own. With his mother gone it would have stirred up more trouble than he wanted. He later learned the truth. From that day on, he chose to look out for him whenever he could. The first time he knew things were bad was when he found him at Tommy's Café in the early hours of the morning. That was the beginning of the relationship he formed with him.

He soon learned that every time his father got drunk, Jack would sleep on the streets. He would find anywhere he could lay his head down. Sometimes it was in the church, most of the time he just went from café to café until the owners booted him out. That morning in Tommy's Café he was huddled in a booth.

It was a little after five. Eddie was on his way to work when he spotted him through the window. To say that Jack was cautious would have been an understatement. He was eleven years of age back then. All Eddie could see was the look in the kid's eyes. Anger. Fear. No child should have had to go through that. But there was something he saw. Strength. The kid had it. He didn't ask for handouts and it took a week before he would let Eddie buy him a meal.

Eventually he offered him a bed at his place. At first Jack thought he was a pervert. He even challenged him on it. Eddie laughed.

"Listen, kid. You want to sleep out here. That's fine by me. I'm just telling you there is a warm bed and food in the cupboard. Take it or leave it. I'm not always home. In fact, I leave early in the morning and return by evening. You decide." Eddie handed him a key. He knew he was taking a risk. Kids were known for stealing in this neighborhood. But he knew Jack was different. He'd seen him stick up for a friend of his. There was a moral compass in him that wanted to do what was right even if Roy Gafino eventually distorted it.

A week or two went past before Eddie noticed a few cans of beans and peach chunks were gone from his cupboard. That was followed by bread. He never took much. Just enough.

Then one morning Eddie awoke and came out to find Jack on the sofa. Jack bolted and Eddie laughed. Over time he became more accustomed to seeing him there. Eventually Jack wouldn't stir when he got ready for work.

Trying to get past his rough exterior was tough though. He had built up a wall. It was a means to protect himself. If he kept people at a distance, they wouldn't hurt him. When he finally got Jack to talk about his father, he learned about the beatings and his sister.

Eddie wanted to report it to Child Protective Services but Jack insisted that he didn't say a word. He believed that his father would just take it out on them even further. He was scared. More so for his sister.

For the longest time he didn't do anything, and the beatings continued. And though Jack had become better at avoiding them before they happened, his sister was still getting them.

Once he'd reached the age of sixteen, things took a turn for the worse. Eddie noticed Jack's interest in Gafino. He was drawn to the boxing down at the Pig's Ear. The kid had a natural talent for whopping ass. He had a drive within him that few others had. Perhaps it came from the hate he had toward his father or that he was born with it. But he had a killer instinct that made him win fights. That's what caught the attention of Gafino.

By the time Eddie found out that he was doing errands for money, it was too late. Gafino had hooked him in. It was the only time that Eddie had raised his voice to Jack. He told Jack it was stupid to get involved with Gafino. That he wasn't helping him because he cared. It was all part of building his empire.

Jack wouldn't listen. He was stubborn.

Now he wasn't only getting beaten by his father but he was fighting with kids in the streets. Eddie had a good mind to give him an ultimatum. Walk away from Gafino or he would close his door to him.

But he couldn't do that. That only became even more evident after what happened next. Now maybe it had been the wrong thing to do. It completely went against his better judgment but Eddie took it upon himself to show up at Jack's father's apartment after he'd given Jack a severe beating. Jack's back was cut to bits. He'd used a belt, and the metal had torn into his skin. Jack had fought back. The first time he'd ever turned and planted one on his father. That punch cost him. He'd hit him so hard that a part of his bone was showing.

Eddie found Jack outside his apartment. He was slumped in a heap at the bottom of the stairs. Eddie dumped the groceries in his hands and carried him up.

"It's alright, kid, I've got yah."

Jack didn't even have the strength to make it up the stairs. His legs were cut to bits. His father had beaten him within an inch of his life.

Eddie lost it that night. He'd never felt so much anger.

After he'd tended to Jack's wounds and made sure he was comfortable, he stepped out into the rain that night with only one thing on his mind. Revenge. When he arrived at the home of Jack's father, rage took over and he murdered the man. He'd killed people when he was in the military but it had always been justified as protecting his country. But this was a straight-up murder. Even now, years later. the only way he could justify it in his mind was to remind himself that he was protecting Jack. He was sure that his father would have killed him had he returned.

That night he disposed of Jack's father in the Hudson River. His body was found a week later. He never mentioned it to Jack but he kind of figured that Jack knew. After that night Jack moved in. His sister Milly stayed for a while but was eventually taken into treatment for physical and sexual abuse. Eddie thought he could help, but she was damaged far beyond what Jack was.

Perhaps that's why Eddie understood Jack more than anyone else. He knew where he came from, what he went through, and how easily he had been sucked into the mob life.

Over the following years Jack came and went as he pleased. They never really spoke about his work with Gafino. Though Jack knew he didn't approve. In order to give him some sense that he would be okay, Eddie taught him how to fight. At first it was just a little hand-to-hand combat; a means to protect himself. Then he taught him a combination of Krav Maga and Aikido. With that and boxing, Jack knew how to handle himself with or without a gun. It instilled a sense of confidence in him.

Eventually he got a place of his own and Eddie saw him less. Their conversations were kept to phone calls. Occasionally Jack would send him some money. He didn't need it. In many ways he believed Jack did this to repay the favor. At first he thought he got an apartment because Gafino had told him to stay clear of Eddie. He soon realized that wasn't the case. He figured Jack had started to understand the danger involved with being part of the mob. His association with anyone would mean placing them at risk.

That became even more evident when Jack did time. The only one that visited him in those four years inside was Eddie. He often wondered if the kid would have got through it, had he not shown up. None of Gafino's men including Roy visited him. Prison had taught him what Eddie could never drill into him. The Mafia was not his family. They would cut you off in a heartbeat if they thought for one minute you were going to squeal on them.

Now as Eddie sat across from Milly at his table, he wondered how they might have turned out had he been there for their mother. One thing for sure, they would have never been as damaged as they were. They were good kids and neither of them deserved the life they had been handed. His only consolation was in knowing that Jack was no longer involved. He had finally come to his senses and seen the extent that the mob would go to in order to get what they wanted. There was no loyalty among them. They were cold-bloodied killers.

Milly spoke only occasionally. When she did, it was quiet and short. A yes or a no. She mainly communicated with a head gesture. Though that had been a vast improvement over her years of silence. Once the treatment center started to see an improvement in her, they were open to have Eddie take her out for a weekend. Jack had made a point to never to give out his address to the center. It would have been the first thing the mob would extract from them. Even Eddie had been careful, he gave them an old post office box over in New Jersey, and a phone number to an answering service.

"So Jack will be coming. It'll be nice. We'll head out and watch the ball drop in Times Square. You'll get to see the New Year in with your brother. What do you think about that?"

In her usual fashion she would raise her eyes then

nod.

"You want some more juice?"

She moved her cup over to him.

"Well, how about that?"

It had been the first time he'd seen her respond beyond a nod.

As they sat at the table quietly eating, little did they know the danger that was nearly upon them.

# 5

Friday morning the weather was better than the day before. The sky was a deep ocean blue. Gone was the blustery wind and constant snowfall. However, it was still cold. He leaned out from under his covers and banged on the electrical heater that was starting to give up the ghost. By the time Jack crawled out of bed, Dana had already left him a text. It read:

*What time do you want to leave for New York?*

He flipped on the TV, stumbled into the cramped washroom, and splashed cold water over his face. He'd got used to his small living quarters on the boat. Though the thought of being able to iron things out with Dana and move in with her again was a welcome one.

In the background the news reported on another string of terrorist attacks that had taken place in Europe. It never seemed to end. Jack took a quick shower and then put on a pot of coffee.

As it was percolating, he took out a small duffel bag and filled it within enough clothes to last a couple of days. It was a good eight-hour drive into the city. He knew it would give them plenty of time to chat. They needed to catch up. For the past few months he'd kept himself busy. Sometimes he lost track of the days.

From beneath his bed he pulled out a black suitcase. It was thin because it contained only a Glock 17 and a few magazines. After walking away from his life in the mob, he was going to dispose of it. He didn't imagine he would have much need for it. But he could never quite bring himself to do it. His gun had become a part of who he was. While he didn't always use it back in the city, it was never out of reach.

The thought of returning to the concrete jungle had weighed heavily on his mind. There was risk involved. Even though the streets would be filled with thousands of people looking to see the New Year in, it didn't mean he couldn't be spotted. If anyone from the mob got wind that he was back, it was liable to get dangerous.

He was pretty sure he'd been seen entering and leaving Gafino's. He fully expected them to put two and two together and seek him out for a little payback. The men who had shown up in Rockland after Gafino's death were proof of that. Their attempts to find him were weak at best. He knew the kind of men they sent weren't ready to jeopardize their life. Had they seen him that day, they might have tried to fire off a round or two, but that would have been it. Few of them nowadays would risk their lives the way he used to.

Jack picked his phone up and sent a text to Dana.

*How did you convince Jason?*

She replied almost instantly.

*He doesn't know yet.*

He didn't bother sending a message back. He was

staying out of this. He knew the kid was having issues. Who wouldn't after finding out your dad was a drug dealer, and the mob had killed him. The repercussions of that night would stay with him for a long time. If he had been in Dana's shoes, he might have run for the hills. The fact that she had given him the time of day spoke volumes about the kind of person she was.

As he tossed a pair of shoes into the bag, he thought about what Eddie had planned. Nothing seemed to faze him. Not the police, the mob, or even death itself. In many ways he'd been a lifeline for Jack. He wasn't sure what he would have done without him. His willingness to keep a close eye on Milly had made him wonder if Eddie really was their real father.

He had considered the rumors.

It wasn't that they even looked alike. There were similarities but Milly didn't look anything like him.

* * *

Dana had been pacing back and forth for the past five minutes. Jason had returned late that night. His frequent trips out with these guys were starting to worry her. Then to have Jack tell her where he'd found him. It had been too much. Jason just wouldn't listen. It was if everything she said went over his head. She was worried that one day she would get a phone call that he had overdosed. He said he wasn't using, but she had her doubts about that.

She knew things weren't right after he stopped showing up for his job. When he turned sixteen, he'd taken a job working at the local supermarket. He'd only been there two weeks when Bob Diamond got in contact to say that Jason hadn't shown up for his past two shifts. She knew right then something was amiss. He hated her rooting around in his room, but the day she came across the paraphernalia and the wads of cash, she was just cleaning up. He had three rolls. In total, it came to over three thousand dollars.

Flashbacks of Matt's involvement in drug dealing came rushing in. She felt her chest become heavy. That was the beginning of the arguments. For a while when

Jack was around, Jason was doing good. Of course, he had his days when he had an attitude but nothing that would have given cause for alarm. Since Jack had moved back to his boat everything had gone downhill. It seemed without a male figure in his life, Jason was prone to go off the rails.

"What time did you get in last night?" Dana asked Jason.

He shrugged. "I dunno."

She stared at him as he crossed the kitchen and grabbed a bowl and a box of cereal from the cupboard.

She tapped her fingers against the granite countertop. "I want to talk about last night."

Jason groaned. "I just woke up, can't this wait?"

"No."

"Look, I'm not going to rehash it."

"I don't get it, Jason. Why? Why go down that road? You saw the way it ended for your father."

"You are starting to sound a lot like Jack."

"Jason, you are sixteen. While you are under this

roof, you will return home when I tell you to."

He remained silent, continuing to pour milk. As he took a seat, she couldn't take it anymore. She slammed her open hand down on the table. She hit it with such force that the milk from his cereal spilled over the brim of the bowl.

"Are you listening?" she yelled.

With that he just turned and left the room. She had never felt this out of control. She charged after him. By the time she reached the top of the stairs he was already in his room with his music blaring. Dana burst through the door and pulled the plug on the unit.

Jason bolted upright with his hands out. "What do you want?"

"I want my kid back."

There was silence.

Jason stared apathetically at her, then sighed before lying back on his bed.

"Listen, I know it's not been easy."

Jason rolled a small stress relief beanbag in his

hand. "Why did you kick him out?"

"Who? Jack?"

"Who else?"

"I didn't. We just thought it would be best. His involvement in helping people around here hasn't exactly been seen as *helping* by everyone. After your father and everything that's happened, I just…"

"You're scared, aren't you?"

"Yeah."

"Is that why you want to move?" Jason asked.

She shook her head and took a seat on the edge of his bed.

"I just want to do what's best for us. We don't have the hotel to worry about now."

"But I thought you liked it here."

"Oh hon, I do. But there's just too many bad memories."

"And what about Jack? You just going to walk away from him too?"

"I don't know." She sighed. "He's invited us to

spend New Year's Eve in New York with him."

"But that's… like tomorrow?"

"Yeah, he wants to leave today."

"And you were going to tell me… when?"

"Do you have something better to do?" she asked.

"No, but…"

"You like Jack, yeah?"

He smirked. "Yeah, he's alright… for a mobster."

She shook her head and let out a chuckle. She patted his leg before jumping up.

"C'mon, I'll make us a proper breakfast, then we'll get our bags packed."

"I have a couple of things I need to do after breakfast."

Dana raised an eyebrow.

"No. Nothing illegal." He tried to reassure her. "I just have to drop by Rachael's place."

"All right, but make it quick. I don't want to keep him waiting."

"When are we leaving?"

"Good question," she replied.

* * *

After breakfast Jason got a ride with Danny Regan back into town. His mother glared out the window as the sports car tore up the gravel and charged off across the breakwater. Danny wasn't just ruining her child, he was destroying her driveway. She would have told him to his face if he wasn't in such a hurry to leave.

Danny was the older brother of Rachael. He was twenty-one. He'd never worked a day in his life. Well, if you could call selling drugs, work. That's how Jason got to know him. He'd been dating Rachael for close to eight months. It was the first steady girl he'd had. Prior to that he'd been with a few other girls but it hadn't lasted.

At first when Jason learned they were dealing drugs, and that Rachael was using he had second thoughts about continuing to see her. But as usual she convinced him that she was trying to kick the habit. But it wasn't just that. In all honesty her brother scared him.

He'd seen Danny put a kid in the hospital using

nothing but his bare knuckles. The guy went by the nickname Meat Sticks. No idea how he got the name. He'd been selling for Danny since the beginning. He'd brought more money in than anyone else, and by all accounts he was considered one of Danny's closest friends.

Problem was, he thought it would be okay to skim off the top.

It didn't take long for Danny to figure it out.

That same evening Danny had made sure that everyone who distributed drugs for him was there. Jason knew something was going down because Rachael had been bouncing off the walls about it all that day. She was hyped up and seemed to feed off her brother's power over others.

"He's going to kick his fucking ass. This is going to be something else."

Jason just assumed he would knock the kid about a bit. Make him embarrassed in front of the others and give him a black eye. He never imagined it would end with the kid on a life support machine. The worst part — he got away with it as no one said anything. That was the kind of power he held over other teens in the town.

Everyone sold for their own reasons. For some it was a way to feed their own drug habit. For others it was a power trip. Having Danny Regan on your side meant no one would touch you. But for most, it was all about the money. And oh, how the money had been flowing.

There really wasn't anything to it. Danny handed out a bag every Sunday evening. He called it his goodie bag. It was filled with a variety of drugs. Weed, LSD, cocaine, speed, and heroin. Everyone knew the danger of getting caught with it on them that's why some came up with creative ways of stashing it. There was one kid who shoved the bag up his ass, and would only deal out of the school toilets. That seemed a little extreme. Kind of sick as well. The truth was, Jason never imagined it would sell. Of course he knew about kids smoking weed, but heroin? LSD? Crack?

The entire bag Danny had given him was gone by

the end of the first day.

That was the moment he knew there was money to be made. It was just too simple. Too tempting.

And so was Rachael. He wasn't sure which had more power over him. The money or Rachael.

"So you got the money?" Danny asked. A cigarette hung from the corner of his mouth. Rachael sat in the back seat with Marko. Marko was a complete freak. Marko wouldn't have thought twice about slashing anyone from ear to ear. There wasn't a day Jason hadn't seen him on drugs. He was always wired.

"Yeah," Jason yanked out two rolls of cash and Rachael took it. It took her less than a minute to count it.

"It's all there."

Danny nodded. "You are doing good. Keep it up. Now what's up with this guy? The one that pulled you out?"

"Jack?"

"Yeah, fucking guy is going to end up with a bullet in his skull."

"Trust me, you don't want to do that."

Danny swerved hard to the side of the road.

"What did you say?"

"I said, you don't want to do that."

"So you are telling me?"

"I didn't mean it like that," Jason replied. He could feel a lump form in his throat. Now any normal person would have asked why. Not Danny.

"Danny, he was just explaining," Rachael added.

"Shut the fuck up." His eyes bore into Jason. "Now is there something you're not telling me?"

"He's seeing my mother."

He burst out laughing. "Oh that's fresh." He pulled back out onto the road. "Mind you, your mother's got quite an ass on her. I wouldn't mind doing her myself."

Jason locked his jaw tight. If he wasn't so afraid of Danny, he might have said something, instead he remained silent. Marko slapped Jason on the shoulder, joining in the laughter.

"Anyway, as I was saying. He's not the kind of guy

you want to mess with."

"Nor am I," Danny said, acting all macho and shit.

"No, he used to work for the mob."

"What?"

"New York Mafia," Jason replied.

"Well, you are just full of surprises, aren't you, kid?"

With that he put out his cigarette and lit up another using the car lighter. He must have gone through two packs a day as he literally smoked cigarettes back to back. It hadn't exactly helped his smile either. His teeth were yellow.

"Well, he better stay out of our way," Danny said, tapping the steering wheel to the rhythm of the radio.

"You not going to listen to him?" Rachael asked Danny. "You heard him. You have to get out by the end of this week. That's within two days."

"Or what? He's going to whack us?" He roared with laughter again.

"Seemed serious to me," Marko said.

"Oh please. He might have caught us off guard last time, but the next time," he leaned over and tapped the glove compartment. It dropped down to reveal a silver .45 Magnum. "He's going to get his head blown off."

Jason couldn't hold in his laughter.

"Something funny?"

"This guy took out four bikers and two of them had guns. You think you are going to kill him with that?"

"Not me. You."

"What?" Jason stammered.

"I'm not going do it. He'll see me coming. But you, nah, he won't know what has hit him," Danny said.

That was how he worked. He always got others to do his dirty work.

"I'm not going to kill him, man."

"Really?"

"No. Are you out of your fucking mind!"

Danny slammed the brakes on. Everyone jerked forward. Inside that car you could have cut the air with a knife. Jason gulped. Danny leaned across, took the revolver and popped out the cylinder with a flick of the wrist. He emptied out the golden bullets into one hand then inserted one bullet. The car idled and Jason glanced over his shoulder at Rachael. She looked back at him. Danny spun the cylinder before flicking it back into place. He cocked the gun and lifted it up to Jason's head.

Jason's mouth went dry, he could feel his pulse beginning to race.

"Danny, stop messing around," Rachael said.

Jason could hear Marko in the back snickering to himself.

"Danny."

"If I have to tell you one more time to shut up, Rachael, I swear I will put a bullet in you." He paused. "Now Jason here wants to know if I'm out of my fucking mind. Well let's see, shall we?"

Jason squeezed his eyes tight. Click. The sound of the cylinder turning over was all it took. He flinched. Nothing had happened. He let out his breath in short bursts, not realizing he'd been holding his breath. He couldn't believe it. He'd pulled the fucking trigger. Jason was literally shaking, unable to even form words.

"Of course I'm out of my fucking mind."

He started laughing and tapped the revolver's barrel on the side of Jason's cheek before tossing it in the glove compartment.

"Man, you should have seen your face."

Marko roared with laughter.

With that he pulled away as though nothing had happened.

# 6

Two hours later Jack arrived at Dana's. They planned to leave at eleven. As long as the traffic wasn't busy they would arrive in the city at around nine that evening. He'd already told Eddie they wouldn't be visiting until the following day. They were liable to be wiped out after the long drive and it would give him a chance to relax with Dana. She was busy filling the back of her truck with a couple of bags when he killed the engine.

"Need a hand?" he asked.

"No, I think I've got everything."

She wiped dirt from her hands and placed a bag of food and water in the front seat.

"Did you see Jason on the way?"

"No." Jack frowned. "He's not here?"

"He said he had to see his girlfriend before he left."

"At least you managed to convince him."

"Barely."

Jack glanced at his watch. They still had another two hours before they would need to get on the road. He suggested they have a bite to eat, probably by then Jason would be back.

* * *

The journey to Rachael's place had been tense. She hadn't said a word. Jason honestly thought she was as scared of her brother as much as anyone else. It wasn't that Danny was physically threatening. He barely had enough meat on him to keep him alive. But you never quite knew what he was going to do. There was always this air of unpredictability surrounding him.

Danny and Rachael Regan had moved to Rockland Cove two years ago with their father. The guy was never around. He was a traveling salesman, so he spent only a few weeks a year at home. That's how they managed to get away with so much. There was no one supervising them or giving them the heavy. Rachael was the same age as Jason. They attended the same school. Jason could never quite figure out what she saw in him. At times he wondered if Danny was behind it. She had done the rounds in school. Most guys looked at her as if she was a bit of a slut. Word had it that she had slept with nearly everyone on the football team. The strange thing was everyone she hooked up with usually ended up dealing or hooked on drugs. Either way they ended up making them money. It was almost like Danny was using her as bait in order to recruit.

In many ways she didn't look like a slut. She could have easily passed for a girl who was part of a chess club. However, she was extensively easy on the eyes and she definitely used her sexuality to lure in guys.

"Why do you let him get away with that shit?"

"What do you expect me to do? He's always been like that."

"And your father? Is he like that?"

Jason had yet to meet her father. Allan Regan. Apparently after their mother had died from cancer, he threw himself into his work. He was rarely home and when he was, Rachael would say that he just stared off into space, or drank until he passed out. It was better with him gone, at least that's what she thought.

She was messed up, but then so was Jason. Perhaps it was because both of them had lost a parent that they connected. Life wasn't exactly as they portrayed it in the movies; happy families, big homes, everyone holding down great jobs. It had been one thing after the next for both of them. Before moving to Rockland Cove, the two of them had lived in New York City.

So when Danny had learned that was where Jason was heading for the weekend, he was ecstatic. Apparently one of his drug connections lived there. Usually they would receive shipments. Drugs came in the same way they used to when Jason's father was involved — by boat. Nothing slowed it down. If one person couldn't bring them, someone else took over.

Problem was, there had been some drugs that had got lost in shipment. They had promised to send more to make up for the loss but they hadn't. That's where Jason came in. Danny wanted him to drop by his contact's apartment in the city and do a pickup.

"I don't think I can do this. Your brother has clearly lost the plot. He wants me to be his drug mule and kill Jack? Are you fucking kidding me?"

"Listen, just pick up the drugs. I'll talk him down on the whole killing. Don't worry about it. I'll make him see reason."

"You better, Rachael, as this is way over my head. I don't mind selling a few blunts here and there at school. But I'm already selling shit that could get me put away for years. My mother has already found the paraphernalia."

"Oh yeah, what did she say?

"What do you think? She went ape shit."

"So you want to back out?"

He stared at her. There was something very disarming about her. Like he didn't want to let her down.

But he knew that wasn't the truth. He just didn't want to lose her. He had fallen for her hard. She had been the first long-term girl he'd had for quite some time. However, he kind of figured she wasn't taking it as seriously as he was. He'd seen her eyeing up other guys. He wasn't stupid. She was the kind of girl that needed the attention. She thrived on being the center of conversation. Why she got involved with him was anyone's guess. He didn't exactly have connections with anyone in school.

"There has got to be a better way to earn money without all the risk and danger involved in this."

Danny had started selling a year ago. At first it was just him getting weed. Rachael would then sell it at school. It didn't take long for greed to get the better of him. Within a matter of months, he'd shifted into the hard stuff and made more money than most corporate employees do in a year. That's when he made the decision to pay for a condo. But he was getting sloppy. His greed was starting to attract the cops. Numerous times they had shown up at condo 112 on Carlton Street. Somehow he always managed to talk his way out of it.

After that he stopped paying for the apartment. He honestly thought he could pay Keith in drugs. But Keith was as clean as a whistle. And now he had Jack looking into things. That was a bad combination.

"This is only going to end badly, and you know it," Jason said.

"You need to relax, Jason."

Rachael laid him back on the bed and begun undoing her shirt. That was her answer to everything. Have sex, get high, and repeat the whole process. But it wasn't going to work this time. Selling weed was one thing but being asked to kill someone and bring back large amounts of drugs from the city was another. They were moving into dangerous territory.

"Get off, Rachael."

She was straddling him at the time, forcing his hands onto her breasts. It was what she always did when he started asking her too many questions. Usually it worked but not this time.

He pushed her back until she lost her balance and toppled over onto the floor.

"Are you fucking kidding me?" she said.

"Listen, I like you. I really do. But things are getting out of control. Your brother is going to wind up in jail, and he'll take us all down with him."

"No, you're wrong. We've gone a year doing this. When the cops come around, he has it handled. Not once have they dinged him. They just think it's kids having a good time. And really, that's all it is."

She moved close again and placed her hand on his face, trying to lure him back into her web of lies and deceit. She had been doing it for so long, she had lost sight of what was manipulation.

He loved her but in this moment he was prepared to walk away from it. He slapped her hand away. As he did, she stumbled over one of Danny's weights and fell on her ass. The look on her face said it all.

She was up fast and he could see that was a bad idea. This whole thing; seeing her, getting involved with them, damn, he had been so stupid. Despite what his mother might have thought, or even Jack, the whole dealing drugs wasn't something that he was keen on. It was a means to an end. A quick way to make enough money to pay his way through college. It beat working at the supermarket. With the hourly salary there he would have had to work for years to get enough to pay for even a year at college.

"Danny," she yelled.

"Oh shit, c'mon, Rachael."

"Danny!"

Danny burst into the room, his eyes looking wild.

"What the fuck is going on here?"

"Seems he thinks he can just walk away from all of this."

"Really?"

Jason raised a hand. "Look, I didn't say I'm walking away from it. It's just this is not me. I'm not a killer, and I certainly don't want to become a drug mule. I thought I could make a few bucks, but I'm no killer, Danny. I like the guy. He's been good to us."

"Oh yeah?" he paused. "Marko!"

Marko came into the room. Danny whispered something to him and he dashed out. Jason was starting to get nervous, his eyes scanned the room for some way out. There was no way out. He pushed forward and Danny knocked him back. Marko returned holding drug paraphernalia: a metal spoon, a syringe, a piece of cotton, and a rubber band.

"What the fuck?" Jason stammered.

"You think you can be privy to this, have a little bit of my sister, and then walk away?"

"This is a joke, right?" Jason asked.

Danny moved forward and Jason took a swing at him and knocked him on his ass. Marko was on top of Jason before he could react. He slammed his fist into Jason's face, knocking him back against the wall. He continued pounding with his legs. Until Jason was barely conscious.

"Stop," Rachael said.

"Rachael, I swear I will put you in the ground if you don't shut up," Danny said before wiping blood from the corner of his mouth and getting back to his feet. Before he said any more, he slammed his foot twice into Jason's gut.

"You will do as I fucking say. You understand?"

He followed up with a few more punches to the face.

"I don't want to get on that shit," Jason said, spitting blood.

He'd seen Danny do this several times with people who wanted to get out from selling. It was simple. He made them addicts. That way they had no other choice than to sell to feed their addiction. If they wanted to walk away, now they couldn't.

He'd seen them. It was like he was building an army of addicts. They would do anything to get that next hit. Good guys. Those who had a clean record. Guys who you would have never imagined would have ended up on drugs were now lost.

Jason tried getting up and a final scuffle ensued as he tried to resist. Danny didn't mess around. He hit Jason hard in the mouth several more times until he was flat on the floor.

"Rachael" Jason mumbled. But she wasn't paying any attention. In fact, she walked out. She was just as scared of Danny as he was.

Marko stepped in. His big, overbearing shadow covered Jason. He began to heat up a chunk of rock on the spoon. Danny held his hand over Jason's mouth while Marko rolled up Jason's sleeve. A minute, maybe two and then he felt a pinprick. Within seconds he felt warmth flood his body. His eyes rolled back in his head and he succumbed to the effects of the heroin.

* * *

It was closing in on eleven and there was still no sign of Jason. Dana had tried his phone several times but got no answer. He'd been gone for almost two hours.

"You think he's bailed?"

"No. He seemed up for it."

She tried to reach Rachael on the phone number Jason had given her but didn't receive a reply back.

"You want me to go look for him?"

"No. He should—"

In that moment the sound of a car could be heard pulling into the driveway.

"Ah, that's him. All right. Let's get going," she said.

When they came out, Jason was lying there on the gravel. Jack watched the red sports car peel away.

"Jason?"

He looked up as if he had just awoken from a long nap, except he hadn't. His lip was bleeding and his face was red.

"You okay?" Dana asked.

"Yeah. Just tired."

Jack crouched down by him and held his face in his hands. His pupils were small. That's when he slid up the sleeves on his arms.

"Oh shit."

"What?" Dana replied.

"He's used."

Dana was at a loss for words. Jack went through his pockets and found some additional heroin. He stared off into the distance at the car that was nearly on the other side of the breakwater.

"I'm gonna..."

Dana grabbed his arm. "No, Jack. Leave it. I don't want more trouble. Let's just get him inside.

* * *

An hour later Jason was beginning to feel better.

"You want to tell me what happened?"

Jason shook his head. His eyes dropped to the floor.

"Did you purposely take this?"

He said nothing.

"What about the cut lip?" Dana asked.

"I really don't want to speak about it."

"And this?" Dana pointed to the chunks of heroin rocks laid out on a piece of paper. As soon as Jason saw it he looked away. A part of him wanted to say what had happened. But he knew it would only end in disaster.

Jack would fly off the handle and storm out of there. No doubt Danny would end up dead and then they would be back in the same boat as they were before.

"How many times have you done this before?"

He rubbed his eyes. "I haven't."

"Are you lying?"

"No, Mom."

"I can't believe this. And after we talked this morning."

Jack came close to Dana and whispered in her ear. "Give me a moment with him. Get the rest of the things together and we'll head out."

"But."

"Dana."

She bit down on her lower lip and then left. Jack waited until Dana was out of earshot.

"Now you want to tell me what actually happened?"

"No."

"They did this, didn't they?"

Jason's eyes met his.

"You know these people don't go away. They don't learn, Jason. They only understand one thing."

"I don't want a lecture from you, Jack. If we are going let's just go."

Jason got up and left the room. Jack sat there quietly. For the most part Jack had avoided the drug scene growing up. He'd seen too many of his friends overdose. Of course, they all said they could handle it. They wouldn't get addicted. How naïve. And then there was stealing to support their habit. If they didn't overdose on the stuff, they were shot for stealing from suppliers. No, Jack stuck to bourbon. It was the better of two evils.

He gave them a few minutes before he joined them outside. Dana was hugging Jason. She loved the kid. And if he was honest, he'd grown attached to him. A part of him wanted to go deal with the problem. That's what he was used to. And this group had it coming to them. They weren't going to leave that condo. He knew it. But right now, Dana and Jason needed a break. They needed this more than he did.

They journey to the city was quiet. Jason slept most of the way. Dana took a turn driving while Jack checked in on Eddie. They arranged to see each other for breakfast the next day at nine.

* * *

Their Hilton hotel was located in Brooklyn. It was about three miles from the Brooklyn Bridge. It was a tall brown building that stood out like a sore thumb. Jack circled around looking for a place to park. It felt good to be back in his stomping ground. Yet he was mindful not to linger long outside. As he searched for a space, all of them were taken. Even the handicap spots were filled. He finally found a spot near the back. He parked the Ford truck, and they rolled in the luggage.

The lobby was a hive of activity. His eyes scanned the crowd for anyone he knew. He would be lying to say he wasn't feeling a little nervous. It wasn't his safety that he was worried about as much as it was Dana and Jason's. A large group of old people were milling around. They must have been there for a convention. The three of them made their way to the check-in and waited in line for a concierge to come over and take the bags.

"I still can't believe you never came to the city," he said to Dana.

"I wanted to but Matt wouldn't have it. He said it would interfere with his business. Obviously now I understand why."

"Did you grow up near here?" Jason asked.

"Yeah, not too far from here. I'll take you there tomorrow."

Jack had reserved two rooms. One for him and the other for Dana and Jason. He could have got one with two king beds but Dana felt it was probably best to keep things separate.

They received their key cards and left the front desk. Within a few minutes they were upstairs and entering the rooms. Both of their rooms were connected by a single door. Jack had insisted they get two rooms together. The thought of being anywhere near the criminal underbelly of New York was disturbing. If he had his way, he wouldn't even step foot in the city. Too many people knew him here. The repercussions of that night at the Pig's Ear replayed in his mind as he unpacked. He hoped to God he didn't run into any of Gafino's associates.

# 7

Eddie Carmine lived in an apartment above a tailor's on Kingsland Avenue in Brooklyn. It was a new residence. He'd originally been living in New Jersey but after everything that had taken place with Jack and Gafino, he moved. It was closer to his work. It wasn't a large place. There were two bedrooms, a small open kitchen, and enough room in the living area for a sofa and chair. He'd never been a man for comforts. His time in the military had taught him to stay vigilant. Long after he was out, he still maintained many of the principles he'd learned in the Marine Corps. He didn't travel far for groceries. He could step outside of his apartment, turn left and walk past two stores, and have access to a full grocery store. There were only two ways out of his place. The main door and the roof. His place was one of three apartments that were above the store. Anyone who wanted to get in needed to ring a buzzer. He'd also installed a security camera. It was hooked up to his TV. A flick of the switch and he could see who was buzzing. He'd avoided numerous door-to-door salesmen this way. But it wasn't salesmen he was concerned about. It was the mob.

Thankfully, in the year that he'd been here, he'd had no visits from anyone. The landlord showed up once every two weeks for his money, besides that he rarely saw anyone come to his door. He liked it that way. He had no brothers or sisters. No family. His father and mother had passed away back when he was in the military. He had learned to enjoy his own company. It was rare that he felt alone. The times he did, he frequented a local escort service. Though that had become less over the past six months.

After life in the military he had no idea of what he

wanted to do. Most of his buddies had become police officers. Some who had specialized in medicine went on to become doctors. None of that had been his thing. He had been trained as a sniper, specializing in explosives and the art of killing. That was all he was good for.

The first few years Eddie had struggled to readjust to civilian life. He took a job at the local auto parts factory creating lights for cars. It was assembly line work. Shift work that was monotonous, and soul destroying. It meant early mornings and late nights. But it gave him time to think. It might have stayed that way if he hadn't read a local article about an increase in stalkers.

They had featured a case about a local businesswoman who was still dealing with a stalker and had reported not receiving much help from police. In the article it raised the question: Was the criminal system letting some offenders slip through the cracks?

It seemed she had pursued action against the stalker and got a restraining order but that still hadn't stopped him from attempting to kill her. Thinking that maybe he could help, Eddie got in touch with her. Perhaps it had been foolish to think he could help, but he did a lot of foolish things when he was younger. He offered to put a stop to the stalker for a price. It was enough money to cover him for two months. She took it.

Two days later the stalker was found dead on the subway tracks. It was ruled a suicide, but the woman knew better. She never said a word. The following sixteen years were filled with jobs helping people. All the while he watched Jack's life from a distance. It was good money. In his mind, he was clearing the scum from the streets. Bringing justice where there was none. He never told anyone. Not even Jack. Eddie planned to keep it that way. Most believed that he still worked for the factory, and for a time he did. It was a nice cover for his extracurricular activities.

He placed another matchstick on the boat he was making. He'd often dreamed about buying his own sailboat and living on the ocean. He was closing in on sixty years of age and while his current means of income made sure that he didn't want for anything; he knew his body couldn't handle the punishment it was taking. Not all the jobs went as smoothly as the first one. He had been stabbed, slashed, and beaten numerous times over those years. One time he was even shot. And still he continued to go out there and help others. Though as the years went on he became more cautious; more picky about the kind of jobs he took. But it was always the same. He would scan the local paper looking for reports on crime, listen to the police scanner, and in most recent years use the Internet.

He looked for cases where anyone had been let down by the system.

Over time most of the jobs he got were by word of mouth.

There were many times he wished he could have told Jack. He'd thought about having him work alongside him but he knew Gafino wouldn't have let him go. He needed that wake-up call. To see Gafino for who he was. Someone who was only out to line his own pockets.

The evening had been like the two before. He'd ordered in Chinese and he and Milly ate it while watching an old Western movie. It was the first time she had tasted Chinese noodles. It was hard for him to comprehend that she had never tasted Chinese food. But then again she had been in treatment since she was eleven.

Over the past year when he visited her, Jack would Facetime. It was the best they could do under the circumstances. After the explosion at the Pig's Ear the city had been crawling with police. He'd seen them coming out of the local restaurants that were owned by the mob. They weren't going to lie down and let the mob set the city on fire.

He'd received a text from Jack that evening to say they had arrived safely and that he was looking forward to seeing them.

The clock ticked quietly in the background. Milly had turned in for the night and he was sitting working on the one hobby that he had taken up since leaving the military. Building things out of matchsticks. It was therapeutic. It focused his mind and calmed him. He would have never got into doing it had it not been for Jack. Jack was shit at buying gifts, and for a while he thought he had come up with another doozy when he handed him the gift on his birthday. Beneath the wrapping paper was a craft set. The Leaning Tower of Pisa. The entire thing had to be constructed out of cardboard and matchsticks.

As Eddie sat there gluing on another stick to the cardboard his mind drifted back.

"What? It will keep you busy in your old age," Jack had said.

"Matchsticks?"

"They say it helps with memory."

"Last year it was a pair of socks. You have outdone yourself."

Jack chuckled to himself.

"Well, you can always make it and then use it for target practice."

"I might just do that."

His mind snapped back into the present at the sound of a buzzer going off. Still holding a plastic bottle of glue in one hand, and a match in the other, he glanced at his watch. It was a little after eleven at night. Had Jack decided to show up early? He reached for the TV clicker and punched it on. The image was unclear at night. There were no lights. But he could make out two men standing in the darkness. Their silhouette said enough. They were bulky and gazing up at the camera. They pressed the buzzer again.

Moving fast, Eddie went over to a cabinet and pressed a button on the side of it. What should have been a place for storing bottles of drink held something far more dangerous. Weapons. He had an AR-15 and two Glock 17s. As he grabbed the two Glocks he heard the sound of a door being broken. He cast a glance at the TV and noticed the two men were now gone but the door was swinging in the wind.

A long staircase led up to a short landing. He could hear the thump of their boots as they came up the stairs.

Eddie dashed into the spare bedroom and woke up Milly. She still hadn't fully recovered from all that she'd endured over the years. They had made progress but it was minimal. This was liable to set her back years.

Eddie guided her into a closet and locked the door behind her. He knew it was futile, but he had to hope they wouldn't look there.

How had they found him? He'd been careful. The phone number he'd given out was for an online software application that then forwarded all his calls to a disposable cell phone. He changed that mobile every month. There was no way someone could find him. Unless he had been spotted, or someone knew his whereabouts. Everything he did was precise. The places he visited. The food he ate. The times he left and returned. He spoke to very few people. The fewer people who knew him the better. Even when he showed up to pick up Milly, he never went in. He avoided cameras.

He racked his brain for answers as he prepared for them to burst through his door.

He didn't have time to figure out how, all he could do was fend them off. He heard a foot pound against the other side of the door.

He raised his gun to heart level. He waited. He wasn't just going to start randomly shooting through the door. He'd triple bolted that door, installed a steel door kick plate. If they wanted in, they were going to have to do more than give it a kick.

The pounding on the door was followed by silence, then rapid gunfire.

# 8

By the time Frank Banfield arrived at the scene he was already feeling agitated. After going over the crime scene down at the East Star Behavioral Treatment Center he was trying to make sense of what seemed like another senseless crime. The initial thoughts by the officers on scene were that it had been committed by addicts.

It hadn't been the first time that their guys had been called out to a treatment center. Most drug users in the city knew that they could find pharmaceutical medication to feed their habit. Trouble was the storage room that held medication hadn't been touched. Usually it would have shown signs of forced entry. Nothing. Then there was the fact they had damaged the surveillance equipment. It just didn't add up.

He had barely got a few hours' sleep when he got another call.

A cup of coffee in hand, he showed up in Brooklyn in the early hours of the morning. A crowd had gathered outside a small block of apartments. Lights from two police vehicles were flashing intermittently. Officers on scene had taped off the area and were keeping a few of the bums back.

"What we got, Carl?"

"One dead. The place has been torn apart. Bum over there said he saw two men bust in the front door before he heard gunfire."

Frank glanced over at a guy in his late fifties. The city was full of them. Their faces and clothes dirty with the grime of the streets. Most were addicted to crack or meth. Some of them slept in cardboard boxes or found warm spots around the city where they could sleep until they were moved along. The sad cases were the former Wall Street brokers. People who had seen the bottom drop out in the late eighties. Those guys had been at the top of their game. Most had owned two homes, boats and vacationed two months of the year. Now they were showing up at homeless shelters.

Frank ducked under the tape and went up the stairs, two at a time. He was closing in on forty. Was still in pretty good shape. You had to be for this job. Too many officers after getting out of the academy let themselves go. But that's why so many criminals got away. They could outrun an overweight, sweating, donut eating cop. He made sure that wasn't the case with him. Whether he had been up all night or not, he was awake by five every morning. He took thirty minutes to work out at his home. That was followed by a thirty-minute jog in the city. It awoke his senses. It got him in touch with those living on the streets. He would see the homeless curled up on benches as he dashed through Central Park or Washington Square Park. Some days he couldn't squeeze in the run, but he always got in that workout.

At the top of the stairs an officer stood watch in the

doorway of the apartment. Inside, CSI were already taking photographs and collecting physical evidence. Lying face down on the floor in a pool of a blood was a body.

"Who is it?"

Tom Parnor was crouched down beside the body, performing an examination. He'd pulled out a wallet with some identification.

"Eddie Carmine. Shot point-blank. Execution style. But not before he had taken one hell of a beating. Whoever did this, tortured him. They pulled out teeth, broke his fingers, put two bullets in his kneecaps."

Frank screwed up his face. The name rang a bell. Carmine? He came around and stepped in close so he could get a better look at the victim's face. He used a pen from his top pocket to lift back the strands of long hair that were obscuring the face. He tilted his head.

"Shit."

"You know him?"

Frank nodded. "Yeah, well, when I was a kid."

An investigator came up from downstairs.

"Frank."

Frank got up and walked over to the main door.

"Seems we might have a possible kidnapping. A witness said they saw the two men leave with a woman. There was a lot of screaming."

"Any description?"

"Too dark but they could hear her."

The next few hours CSI gathered what evidence they could collect. Trying to solve these kinds of crimes was like searching for a needle in a haystack. It wasn't just the fact they happened so often. Witnesses were usually too scared to speak. Those who did were usually bums. Most of the time their accounts were sketchy at best as they were just keen on getting cigarettes and coffee in exchange for information. Then when you gave them what they were after, they would just come up with anything. It was like chasing your own tail.

# 9

Seven o'clock in the morning was always a busy time in the city. The city never rested. It was stunningly beautiful outside that morning. From the hotel window Jack could see pedestrians already clogging up the sidewalks and yellow taxis honking for no other reason than they were New Yorkers. The tree branches of Central Park would have been coated in a deep frost, not that he could see them from Brooklyn but he had made a mental note to take Dana and Jason there before they returned to Rockland Cove. The concrete jungle beyond the window was as stunning as he remembered.

He had a bounce in his step that morning. It was New Year's Eve. The time of the year that the city came alive. The best time to visit the city and go unnoticed. And yet the one time of the year people could vanish unnoticed.

Jack found the fresh air intoxicating as he returned to the hotel that morning with a tray of coffee. He could have purchased it from the lobby, or even made some in his room, but he knew the area, and remembered a local café that had been a favorite of his. It was a little after seven when he entered the warmth of the lobby.

It had been over a year since he'd seen his sister in person. Talking via a mobile device always felt uncomfortable. He'd specifically chosen a hotel that was a little rundown. Nothing fancy. Nothing that might draw attention. It was odd being back in his old stomping grounds. He thought of the many people he had killed in Brooklyn. Those he had taken and dropped to the bottom of the Hudson River. Life in the mob was something that few would ever understand. Why would a person get involved? People did not choose it. You were chosen. They were very picky about who they brought into their inner circle. Most of them had grown up in families that were already involved. He'd once overheard someone talking in a bar. A tourist about the recent string of arrests. Why wouldn't they just leave? Why not just walk away? You didn't walk away from the mob, by the time you were involved it just became a way of life. After you got away with murder once, twice, even three times, you started to think you were untouchable. Then, add to that the money that flowed like water and the comradery. It felt like a brotherhood. But that's how it appeared on the surface. That's what most thought it was until they were staring down the barrel of a gun, until they were ratted on. Then the tables turned, and it showed its true face.

Jack knocked on Dana's door and Jason answered it. He handed him the tray. He could hear the shower going. Jason said she'd been in there for over twenty minutes. That might have been cause for concern if it wasn't for the fact that Jack had lived with Dana for several months and had witnessed her lengthy bathroom routine.

"You think you two might want to have some alone time today?"

"What?"

"You know, show her the sights."

"What about you?"

"I was just thinking of chilling here. Going in the pool, maybe stepping out and browsing some local stores."

Jack chuckled. "There is a really big music store about four blocks from here, you might want to check it out. They have tons of drums."

"Sounds like a plan."

"You don't want to come with us this morning?"

"Nah, as much as I would like to meet your sister and all, I'm really not feeling too good."

"But good enough to go visit a music store?"

Jack smirked.

Dana came out of the bathroom. She was already dressed and looking gorgeous like usual. Her hair was up, she wore tight jeans, and a form-fitting red shirt.

"Jack?"

He handed her a coffee.

"Ah, you are a saint."

He laughed. "Some might argue with that."

"So what time do you want to head over?"

"I thought I could take you over to Central Park first. Watch the people ice skate. Try it out if you like."

"Ice skate? Me, no I will end up on my ass."

"Then we'll take a walk. I'll show you the sights."

"I'd like that."

"Though you might want to talk to your boy here, he doesn't seem up for it."

"Jason?"

"I'm really not feeling too good."

"Maybe I should stay back?"

"No, you go out. Have some fun. I don't want to ruin it."

"All right but we'll check back in later with you, okay? Before we head over to Jack's sister's."

"You have enough money on you? Just in case you need anything?" Jack asked.

Jason chuckled.

"Right."

They both knew he had more than enough with what he'd earned from selling drugs.

"Listen, you get into any trouble, you call this number, okay?" Jack tapped his number into Jason's cell.

Ten minutes later they were out the door but not before Jack retrieved his gun from his room. He strapped it underneath his jacket. He wasn't taking any chances. Dana was still concerned about leaving Jason behind but Jack reassured her that the place was safe even if that was a lie. Fact was the mob was everywhere, they owned a piece of every neighborhood and what they didn't own, they collected in protection money from local businesses.

They caught a taxi from Brooklyn over to Central Park. It was a crazy amount of money but it was better than getting stuck on the subway at this time of year. The taxi guys knew their way around this city better than most locals. And with New Year's Eve about to kick off, the place was about to be infested by over one million people in Times Square alone. It was a crazy time of the year to show up in the city. But Jack was hopeful that it would go well. In two days' time they would be back in Rockland Cove and away from all the danger. How Eddie had managed to talk him into showing up here was anyone's guess. He could convince an Arab to buy sand.

As they traveled through the streets, Dana gazed out the window and marveled at all the sights. Jack pointed out places he used to visit. Good places to eat and some areas you didn't want to go into but most tourists did. Usually the best way to get around was by subway. You could go from one end of Manhattan down to the other in a matter of ten minutes.

There was a buzz to the city. An energy that you felt as you walked around and squeezed your way through the crowd. Some people gazed at you, others wouldn't even look. People were busy shopping, others mesmerized by the neon lights that dripped with hope and materialism. Buy this, buy that. Everything was for sale. Clothes, food, sex, and drugs. If you knew where to look you could get what you wanted. It was in many ways a buffet that was laid out. A tasty array of flavors served up into trays. Little Italy, Chinatown, SoHo, and much more. There was never a dull moment. You could spend days seeing the sights. Most would have to spend several weeks just to take in all the attractions. But it was what most didn't see that really appealed to Jack. The underbelly of the city. The deals that occurred in the back of shops. The money that was extorted, the crooked arrangements that were made in dark alleys.

For many of those who grew up in the city, this was the attraction. This is what pulled them in. The chance to make a name for themselves and run with the big dogs. The ones who pulled the strings and governed the affairs of others. They were judge, jury, and executioner. They didn't answer to the police. The police answered to them if you paid them enough. And everyone had a price. It didn't matter who you were. From lawyers to judges and police. There was virtually no one that had a clean record in this city. The only one he could remember who didn't touch any of it was Frank Banfield. He had admired him since they had met.

In many ways Jack had even envied his life. He imagined that Frank was what he could have become had he turned away from a life of crime. Who knew, maybe by now he would have had his own family, kids too. But that wasn't Frank. Jack had watched his life from the sidelines. Their friendship had gone in very different directions by the time he was running with Gafino. Over the years Frank had got close to nailing Jack. Thankfully Jack had always been one step ahead. Making sure that nothing was left behind that could incriminate him. Though he had got sloppy over the years as he had grown older. Thirty-nine wasn't old but in his line of work it meant he had to be more careful.

Yeah, the city was full of all types. The good, the bad, and the ugly. After they had walked for a good hour around Central Park and some shops they made their way back. It didn't take long to get tired in the city. Your senses were attacked by lights, noise, and the pull of the next attraction.

Upon returning to the hotel they found a note saying that Jason had ducked out and would be back in a couple of hours. If they needed to find him, he would likely be down at the music store, the one that Jack had mentioned.

Sure enough, on their way over to Eddie's they swung by the store and peered in. There he was banging away on drums and chatting with a sales rep.

Satisfied that he was okay, they continued on their way. It wasn't far. Maybe ten minutes at most. When they turned the corner that led up to Eddie's, Jack's stomach sank. His mouth went dry, and he felt his pulse beginning to race. It wasn't just that the police were in the area. Police were seen all over the city at this time of the year. It was the fact that Frank Banfield was on the scene and that meant only one thing. Someone was dead.

# 10

Jack tapped the taxi driver on the shoulder and told him to stop. He paused for a minute trying to contemplate whether to get out or have the driver turn around. He had no idea what the police had on him regarding the death of Gafino. He could find himself back in the slammer. There was no way he was going back to Rikers. It had almost killed him the first time.

"What is it, Jack?" Dana asked.

"Are you getting out or do you want to go somewhere else? I've got a business to run," the taxi driver said.

"Just give me a minute," he replied.

He stared into the crowd of people gathered outside. It had been years since he'd seen Frank. Frank was speaking with an officer when he glanced their way. He wouldn't have been able to see who they were as they were in the back seat of the taxi and a block away. However, he might think it was a little strange that a taxi was idling on a road where there were few other vehicles.

"Turn around, let's go," Jack said.

He didn't want to leave. Everything inside of him was screaming. He wanted to get out and see what was going on. His sister. Eddie. He thought about texting him. Shit. They would have his phone. Eddie had always taken precautions. He'd bought disposable phones but with CSI on scene, they had probably removed any computers or cell phones. He had never given his address to Eddie. In his mind the fewer people who knew about the place, the better.

"What's the address?"

"Huh?"

He was still lost in thought. Trying to process what he had seen. He looked out the back window as the taxi did a U-turn in the road and pulled away. Frank had returned to his duties. He wasn't wanted by the police as far as he knew. Eddie hadn't managed to dig up anything, but he wasn't going to take any chances, at least not until he found out what was going on.

"Take us to the East Star Behavioral Treatment Center."

"You got it, boss."

He sat back in his seat with a look of concern on his face.

"Jack, what is going on?" Dana asked.

"I don't know yet. Just."

"Jack, this — "

"Dana, please. I need a moment to think."

His mind was racing with every scenario he could imagine. Had the police finally tracked him down through Eddie? Had the mob arrived first? Or could this have all been a misunderstanding?

* * *

When they arrived at the center, Jack paid the driver and told him to wait. Dana and he went inside. By now things had returned to almost normal. Any sign of the crime that had occurred a few nights ago was gone. It was business as usual though they now had two armed guards on the door. When they approached the front desk, there was an elderly woman in front of them. She was taking forever.

"You think I can…" Jack asked.

The older woman turned. "Young man, you'll have to wait your turn."

"Listen, I just need to know…"

"Sir, just take a seat and we'll be with you in a moment," the attendant said.

Dana tapped Jack's wrist, and they took a seat. Dana was trying to get a hold of Jason by texting him but getting no reply.

"What do you think is going on?"

"Whatever it is, it doesn't feel good. I knew this was a bad idea."

Eventually the woman ahead of them was finished. Jack went to the front desk and enquired about his sister. They pulled up her details and said she wasn't due to be back for another day. Jack thanked the woman. As he was leaving, he glanced up at the camera. He had no idea of what had gone down. Outside, Dana slipped into the taxi. Jack gave the driver some extra money and told him to take her back to the hotel.

"But, Jack?"

"Just go. I need to figure out what's going on with Eddie."

"And Jason?"

"I'll see if I can find him, but for now just go back and don't open the door to anyone."

He could see the look of concern on Dana's face. There was very little he could do right now to alleviate that other than track down Jason and get him back to the hotel. He willed his mind to relax. He had no way of knowing if this was a problem. Something in his gut didn't feel good though.

He watched the taxi drive away before he hailed another one and jumped in. He had the driver take him to the music store just a few blocks from their hotel. When he arrived, he poked his head inside and asked the store owner if he had seen a kid resembling Jason. Like any owner whose focus was on selling, and who probably had seen countless faces that morning, he just shook his head and went back to the business of serving customers.

"Take me to Kingsland Avenue," he next told the driver.

Ten minutes later they were there. He had the taxi driver drop him off a few blocks from the apartment. There was just one cruiser there. Whatever they were doing, they had probably wrapped it up and moved on to the next call. Very rarely did it take them long even if there was a dead body. The New York police were in and out. They didn't have the luxury of a small town where they could linger and shoot the breeze. Besides, they dealt with death on a daily basis. It was routine.

As the taxi pulled away, he took a seat on a set of steps and waited. An hour passed before the cruiser drove away. The place was still taped off when he strolled up there. An old guy and a young kid were outside. They were talking when he came up on them.

"Anyone hurt?"

"They took a body out of here on a stretcher. I'm guessing yeah." The kid had an attitude.

Jack ducked under the tape.

"Hey, you can't go up there," the old man yelled.

Jack didn't listen, he buzzed the door for one of the other apartments.

"Delivery."

The door clicked. Why people still fell for that was beyond him. Within a matter of seconds, he was on the landing. The door to Eddie's apartment was locked. He twisted the handle. As he was doing that one of Eddie's neighbors came out. A black woman with a huge microphone style Afro.

"Darlin', you got business there?"

"Was an old friend," he replied.

"They locked it. You ain't getting in there."

"Did Eddie give you a spare key by any chance?"

He'd done that before with his old place, but Jack wasn't sure how much he would have trusted the folks in this neighborhood.

She shook her head. “Like I said, you ain’t getting in.”

“That’s what I thought.”

He stepped back and with one brute force kick, he hit the door right at the point where the lock met the doorframe. Wood split and the door swung open. He glanced at her.

“Or you could do that,” she said.

She didn’t look fazed by it. Her pupils were dilated. The woman was as high as a kite. Jack knew he didn’t have long. The police could return at any moment. He just had to see for himself.

Inside a patch of dry blood was the only sign of injury. Beyond that the place had been torn apart. Whether the mess had been made by the police or someone else was unknown. Practically anything that would have been any use to him was already taken. Computers, papers, all that remained was what you usually found in any apartment; the furniture, a bed, and kitchen items. It was cramped inside. He tried to replay in his mind what might have happened. He looked at the door. Bullet holes. Six of them. He followed the line of fire across to the wall where the bullets would have entered the drywall. CSI would have taken those. On a side table were a few photos. Nothing that he hadn't seen before in Eddie's last apartment.

He moved into the bedroom, he looked through the drawers. In one was a Bible. A New King James. It was made of dark brown leather. It was an odd thing to see. Eddie wasn't religious. He opened it and flipped through. In the front scribbled in black ink were the words:

*Hope this brings you peace,* John Dalton.

As he was about to place it back in the drawer, a photo slipped out. It looked like a recent photo of Eddie. Behind him, a city. It didn't look like New York as there were palm trees. Beside him was a young man. He was the spitting image of Eddie. But Eddie didn't have kids, did he? He had never mentioned once traveling. Who was this person? Jack ripped the front page out of the Bible and pocketed the photo. He went back out of the room and checked the guest bedroom. That was where Milly would have been. He looked around for anything that belonged to her, but there was nothing. Returning to the living area he went over to the drink cabinet and pressed the button on the side. To anyone else it would look like a typical cabinet. You could even pull down the cupboard door in front and see bottles of alcohol. However, Jack had seen Eddie years ago retrieve a gun from it. The button on the side look like a part of the cabinet, it was built that way so that no one would know. Jack pressed it and a concealed side door flipped down. The handguns were gone but the assault rifle was there. There was no way he was going to be able to walk out of there with it. He ran his hand underneath the shelf inside the hidden compartment and found the keys. Eddie stored anything that was of value in a storage area in New Jersey.

His mind was racing, thinking about what had happened. Someone from the mob might have shown up and Eddie could have taken them out. Worst-case scenario, he'd been shot. Perhaps he wasn't dead. Maybe the old man outside had got it wrong.

Jack turned to leave when he heard the sound of footsteps coming up the stairs. He could have ducked out the window and used the fire escape but with it being a crime scene, he didn't want to give the police reason to chase him. He shut the hidden compartment just as they walked in.

"Jack Winchester."

It was Frank Banfield.

"How did I know you were caught up in this?"

Jack turned around and gave a wry smile.

"Been a long time, Frank. It's got to be, what? Five years?"

"What are you doing here, Jack?"

"I came to see Eddie. I was meant to see him and my sister this morning."

"Where have you been living?"

"Here. There."

Frank strolled over to the window while another police detective stood at the door. Frank looked out and breathed in deeply.

"Eddie is dead."

"What?" Jack replied.

"You know anything about this?"

"What about my sister?" he asked.

"She wasn't here. Whoever killed him took her."

"So she's alive?"

"If our witness is telling the truth, yes."

Jack could feel rage rising in him and a mix of desperation and anger.

"Right, well, I'll leave you to it."

"Can't do that, Jack. I'm going to have to take you down to the station."

"For what?"

"Until we find out what's going on here, you're not just going to disappear again."

"You can't hold me."

"In fact I can. Breaking and entering."

"Oh please, really?"

Frank cocked his head to one side.

* * *

Within a matter of minutes, they had taken him out to an unmarked car and whisked him away to the Midtown South Precinct. Lines of police cars parked at diagonal angles faced the front entrance of a tall brown building. It was one of the most modern-looking police precincts in New York. Not like some rundown ones that looked as if they hadn't seen a lick of paint since the eighties.

Jack was brought into an interrogation room. It was square with a two-way mirror, and a camera. One single table and two chairs.

"Can I get you some coffee?" Frank asked.

"No, I don't plan on staying here long," Jack answered.

Frank chuckled and walked out. He returned five

minutes later. Removed his suit and took a seat.

"Man. It's been a long time. How did it go in Rikers?"

"Slow."

Frank snorted as he flipped through some paperwork in front of him. He twisted around a couple of photos and placed them in front of Jack. Jack immediately recognized them.

"Now for the past year, I've been sitting on these and wondering. Does that look like Jack Winchester?"

Of course it wasn't easy for anyone to recognize who it was as the photos were dark, grainy and hell, he'd seen better photos of unidentified flying objects than these.

"Hard to tell, isn't it?"

"What do you think?" Frank asked.

"I think they need a new camera."

Frank shook his head and threw a few more down in front of him. These however weren't of him. They were of the charred remains of Gafino and several other men that were inside on that night.

"Now we all know that no one is really weeping about the loss of Roy Gafino. He deserved to die. But here I am wondering who might have had a reason to kill him? Better still, who could have got close enough to kill him?"

Jack sniffed. "By the looks of it, no one would have been close. Otherwise they would have been there with him."

"Don't be a smart ass, Jack. Your sister is now missing. We had two homicides at the treatment center, which we figure was done by the same people who killed Eddie."

As he said that he tossed a photo of Eddie Carmine down. Jack squeezed his eyes shut. A flood of memories came back in. He could hear Eddie's voice replaying in his mind from only a day ago, saying he was looking forward to seeing Jack again.

"Now I've got to ask myself how all of this has happened on the same day you return to the city? Do you want to shed some light on that?"

"I wish I could help you."

Frank stared blankly back at him.

# 11

Frank joined another detective on the other side of the two-way mirror.

"So what do you think?"

"Cut him loose," Frank said.

"You don't want to at least keep him in for twenty-four hours?"

"He's better to us out on the streets. We'll tail him, see where he goes."

"You think he knows who did it?"

"I think he has a good idea, and that's what I'm counting on right now."

The other detective nodded.

"How long have you known this guy?"

"A long time," Frank replied, studying Jack.

It was strange to see him after all of these years. To think of the way their lives had changed. Both of them saw the underbelly of New York and lived among criminals. Frank had known what Jack's upbringing was like. Between the ages of nine and sixteen they had formed an unlikely friendship. Frank's own father had grilled him over it numerous times, especially when they were found smoking. Back then it was simple things. Smoking, porno mags, stealing from your local candy store. Nothing that most in the world hadn't done.

However, Frank's father felt that Jack was a bad influence on him. Truth be told, most of the bad ideas came from Frank. It was just Jack who knew how to pull them off. Frank's home was religious, rule-based and most of the time you felt like you were walking on eggshells. Jack's was the complete opposite. He came and went as he pleased. There were many nights he didn't get fed a meal. Frank couldn't count the number of times he had sneaked out food. That was until Jack met Eddie after that things changed. He began spending more time with Eddie. Then once he got into boxing and involved with Gafino, they just drifted apart. He still considered Jack his childhood friend, but they were different now. Worlds apart.

* * *

Jason had spent a good portion of the morning at the music store. He wouldn't be able to meet Danny's connection until noon. Eventually he left and wandered the streets. He walked across the Brooklyn Bridge and caught a subway up and down Manhattan. It felt good to be away from Rockland Cove. His mother trusted him at age sixteen probably more than most parents would. Maybe it was because she was single and expected him to act more grown up.

Truth was since his father's death he had been forced to grow up fast; to become streetwise. He was torn over his relationship with Rachael. The way she had stood by while they injected him with heroin. Most guys would have run for the hills. But there was something in her that he was attracted to. Something that told him she was just a puppet in Danny's game. That she could in some way be saved from it all. That was the only reasoning he could give to why he was seeking out this drug contact. He imagined in his mind that if he could just hang in a little longer that somehow he could persuade Rachael to walk away from it all.

He knew she was tired of following Danny's orders. But like him, she was lacking a father figure in her life. Her own father might as well have been dead. He was never around. He needed more time to think it through. Find a way to help her to see that her involvement with Danny was only going to lead to a prison sentence. He would need her to get off that shit too. But now he had tasted it himself. And God it felt good. He could see why people got addicted to it. It took away all the pain he felt inside. For a brief few hours he felt as if everything bad that had happened in his life was now a distant memory. Nothing could touch him. It was beautiful, and yet he knew logically it wasn't. It eventually would take you down. Strip you of everything you had and eventually kill you.

When he returned to Brooklyn, he had to head over to a housing estate near Vinegar Hill called Farragut Houses. It was a rundown section of Brooklyn. Tall brown buildings with too many apartments. All Danny had given him was a scrap of paper with an address and a name — Spike.

He was nervous when he showed up there. Outside a group of black teens played basketball. They glared at him as he followed a path that led up to the entrance. One of them broke off and was heading in his direction. He didn't like this one bit. He'd heard of people being mugged in New York all the time. They didn't think twice. They would slash, stab, or shoot you.

He entered the building and took one look at the dirty elevator and opted to take the stairs. As he entered the stairwell he looked at all the graffiti sprayed over the walls. People's tags and obscene images stood out among the grime and bubblegum that covered what used to be white paint. He had to go to the fourteenth floor, apartment 501. He began to climb, realizing this was going to take a while. It smelled like piss and shit inside the stairwell. For a few seconds he had considered leaving. But as he gazed down below, he heard someone come in. He assumed it was the black guy who had broken off from the group of basketball players. On his way up the stairs he saw a couple of kids playing. A mother sat outside. The moment she saw him, she grabbed her kids and dragged them inside. A drunk was asleep on one floor with a brown paper bag covering his liquor. He stepped over the puke that was close by and continued on up.

Behind him he could hear the sound of someone climbing the steps fast. He was only at the sixth floor. Nervous, he ducked into the hallway and waited until he heard them go by. He gave it a minute or two. A dim, sickly looking yellow light flickered above him. He saw several teens down the far end of the hallway coming on to some girl. Everything about this place felt wrong. Like all the worst of New York had been crammed into one building. He went back to the stairwell and continued climbing.

It took him a while to reach the fourteenth floor. Whoever owned this place had not bothered to fix it up. Jason stepped over what was without a doubt piss. To think that someone had stepped into the stairwell to relieve themselves was sick.

When he reached apartment 501, he knocked and looked at the peephole. He had no idea what he was meant to be picking up from them. All he had was a backpack. He didn't expect he would be carrying out large amounts of heroin, or was that the plan? He hoped not.

From outside he heard footsteps approach the door. They paused, obviously someone was looking through the peephole before opening up.

It was the same guy he'd seen from the basketball court.

# 12

Outside the police station, Jack breathed in deeply, casting a glance over his shoulder. He knew they would be following him. The fact that they had released him even though he had broken into Eddie's place was a complete giveaway. He surveyed the area, gazing down at the business card Frank had given him. His number and address were on the back. There were cop cars lined up and several unmarked vehicles. First order of business was making sure they were off his tail.

He sat on the steps to gather his thoughts. Since arriving at Eddie's he hadn't had a chance to think about where he should look. The only thing creeping through his mind was what did they have on him? He didn't want to go back to prison. He wouldn't. With Gafino's crew gone, the only other crime family that would have tried to step into his shoes would have been Leo Carlone's. He couldn't exactly walk in there after killing his son.

Jack wrapped his jacket around him tightly. The wind kicked up snow from snowdrifts. He started heading east, keeping a close eye on the road to see who was following. Within a matter of minutes he caught sight of an unmarked car. They weren't exactly good at staying out of sight. Did they really think they could follow him at this time of the year? There were even more people on the streets in preparation for the New Year's celebrations. As he approached an entrance that led down into the subway, he glanced back and saw the car pull to the side. Not wasting another second he dashed down the stairs and broke into a full sprint. The underground was packed with people coming and going. He felt like a fish trying to go upstream.

He cast a glance over his shoulder. Above the crowd he could see the two men in plain clothes struggling to get through the mass of people. He could hear the sound of a train coming in. He nearly lost his footing as he shot down the stairs. Several New Yorkers cursed him. In a matter of seconds the train would be leaving. As he pushed his way forward, his heart was pounding in his chest. Sweat poured off him.

The doors were closing on the train when he shot through the gap. They sealed shut, and the train pulled away. He glanced at the two men who looked worn out and exasperated.

He slumped down on a torn-up leather seat and breathed a sigh of relief.

* * *

Back at the housing project, Jason had been brought into what initially looked like one apartment. They had patted him down and checked to make sure he didn't have any wires. What he discovered though was they had knocked down the walls between three other apartments beside it and set up the entire place for storing, cutting, and bagging heroin and crack.

Spike was at least six foot three, with an athletic build and a shaved head. He had tattoos all over his body. He introduced him to three people who he called his associates. They were sitting on a sofa. One of them was doing some blow. Jason spotted a handgun on the table.

"So Danny said you had something for me to collect?"

Spike nodded to another guy, and he went into the next room. A few minutes later he came back with two black suitcases. He slammed them on the table and popped the locks. Inside were stacks of heroin. Jason's eyes widened. There was no way in hell he was going to be caught with that amount on him. He had thought it was a small bag, something he could easily stash.

"Give me a second."

Jason made a phone call to Danny. He walked into another room.

"What is it?"

"You never told me how much you wanted me to bring back. I can't bring that back."

"Do you want to repeat what you just said?"

Jason paused. He knew he was walking on eggshells. This was a bad situation. These thugs had guns and all it would take was one word from Danny and he would end up dead.

"Listen, Danny, think about this. I've got to walk across town with these and come up with some excuse to my mother. We are sharing the same suitcase. Do you see what I mean here?"

"Not my problem. You just bring them back or else."

Jason didn't even want to ask what "or else" meant, he knew.

"Now are we good?"

"Yeah," Jason reluctantly replied.

Jason strolled back into the room where the four black guys were talking among themselves.

"Any problem?"

"No," Jason replied. "So I guess I'll be going."

Spike let out a slight laugh. "Are you serious? We

still need payment."

"What? Didn't Danny pay you?"

Spike glanced back at the others. "Are you telling me you showed up here without any green?"

"Danny said I was just picking up. I'm as surprised as you are. I can get him back on the phone."

"Fuck that shit. What the fuck is this?"

Oh shit. This was about to go bad real quick. How could he have sent me in here knowing full well that he hadn't paid them, he thought.

Jason tossed his hands in the air. "Look, I don't know what kind of arrangement you have with Danny but I can reassure you. I was just told to pick up. I'm not involved beyond that."

"Maybe we'll keep you as payment until he sends the money."

Spike pulled a gun from behind his back and placed it against Jason's head. All the color in Jason's face washed out. Fear was the thing overriding his senses.

"Get him on the phone," Spike said.

Jason hit the speed dial then handed the phone to him. Spike kept the gun against his temple while he took the phone.

"What the fuck is this, Danny? We don't owe you shit. In fact, you owe us for that lost shipment."

Jason could barely hear what Danny was saying, but he was close enough that he could just make out the gist of the conversation. It seemed that a package had been lost or taken by the feds. With no money exchanged, Danny felt he was owed a new batch of heroin and wouldn't pay until it arrived. However, Spike didn't see it that way. He thought that maybe Danny was trying to screw them over. He believed that maybe the feds weren't involved, and that Danny had received the package and was now trying to get more.

"I will shoot your boy right here and now."

Jason heard Danny tell him to go ahead. He couldn't believe what he was hearing. God, he had been so stupid to get wrapped up with Danny.

Spike hung up.

"Seems he doesn't give a shit. So we're going to send a message to him and send you back in little pieces."

"Listen, I know Danny has screwed you over. But I swear I didn't know anything about that."

He pressed the gun hard enough against his head that he leaned to one side against the wall.

"Means nothing to me."

"I can get you money. Whatever you need. Just don't shoot me."

Spike glared.

"How?"

"I have a guy. He can have it here within the next hour. I just need to let him know."

Spike handed him the phone. Jason could tell he was a hair's-breadth away from being shot. He took the phone and hit speed dial on the number for Jack. Jack picked up.

"Where are you?" Jack asked.

"You know that thing we were talking about earlier? Yeah, I'm gonna need you to bring it."

"Jason?"

"And within the next hour or I'm going to be eating more than a big apple."

"Where are you?".

# 13

At Leo Carlone's restaurant heated words were being exchanged. Dominick and Anthony had brought Milly back without Leo even giving the go-ahead.

"Are you out of your fucking minds? Why the hell would you bring her here?" Leo said to Vito.

"Leo, you want this man? Then you have to do it our way."

"Your way? Your way is going to get us killed."

"What you have done up to now hasn't worked."

"You don't get it, do you? You honestly don't know who you are dealing with?"

"We know enough to make us question our association with you," Vito replied.

"You just opened a can of worms. He'll come."

"Exactly and when he does, we will be ready."

Leo shook his head. The door to the joint swung open and three of his own men came in. They seemed out of breath.

"We just got word from our guy over at the station that he's in the city. He's staying at a Hilton on the Lower East Side with a woman and her son."

"Dominick, Anthony, go," Vito commanded.

"You aren't…"

"Aren't what? We will do whatever it takes."

The restaurant cleared as Vito's men headed for the hotel.

* * *

It had taken Jack the better part of forty minutes to get over to the apartment block. By midafternoon the city was teeming with people. The celebrations had already begun. Bars were overflowing, and the city was abuzz. He had no idea of what he was walking into, only that whatever Jason had got himself involved in, it was trouble.

He'd cringed when Jason gave him the address. Farragut Houses had been known as a housing project where drug deals were the norm, even five years ago. He'd been out there numerous times when he worked for Gafino. Back then though it was different. Gafino controlled who distributed. They all worked for him in one capacity or another. Most of the foot soldiers, as he liked to call them, answered to one of their own. In their mind he was the boss. But he had a boss, and so did his boss, until you reached Gafino at the top. The DEA were always trying to get to Gafino, and they had come close numerous times. They would bust an operation and offer them a deal. A lesser sentence if they squealed on who they were working for. The problem for the DEA was that the foot soldiers weren't afraid of them. They were terrified of what would happen to them inside the pen for ratting. So many just took the hit, did their time, and the cycle continued.

Only once had Gafino paid Jack to go out to

Farragut Houses and kill someone. He had been running his own business on the side. Most of them wouldn't dare do it. It was usually the ones that were using themselves.

As Jack approached the main entrance he glanced up at the window where it all happened. His thoughts of that day were forever embedded in his mind. He had been twenty-two at the time. He hadn't built a reputation at that point, but in time he would.

When he showed up to collect on the money that was owed to Gafino, a Hispanic man had opened the door. Inside he was met with a scene that made the task difficult. The guy had a wife and three kids there. His wife was pregnant with their fourth child. The whole incident stuck out in his mind because he learned a valuable lesson that night. He still had the wound to show for it. The guy's name was Tomás. He knew immediately why Jack had shown up. He stepped outside and closed the door behind him.

"Not here, please. I don't want them to know."

Back then he would listen to those he was sent to

kill. As the years went on, he stopped listening. Doors would open and he would shoot them and walk away. But when he was younger, he was interested in seeing how they would try to wiggle their way out of a situation they had placed themselves in.

"You've bitten the hand that feeds you, Tomás."

"I know. I know."

"Why?"

"I didn't think he would know. I know, stupid."

"So how do you want to do this?"

Murder seemed strange back then. To think that his job was killing people, or hurting them badly. To ask them how they wanted to go was absurd but for a time that's what Jack would ask.

"The window. I would rather make it look like a suicide."

Tomás led Jack into a separate apartment that he used for dealing drugs out of. No one was inside. A lone table was in the middle of the room. A fine trace of powder remained on the table. As he got closer to the window, Tomás started to get agitated. That's when the pleading started.

It always happened. Some would plead for their lives the moment they laid eyes on Jack. Others would try to act like a man and take what was coming for them only to fall apart in the last few seconds. These were the same scum that had raped, murdered, and tortured other people for far less. For years Jack felt nothing for them. They had dug themselves a grave. He saw his job as merely covering them in dirt. They were dead whether he showed up or not.

Tomás paused at the window, his hands trembling. Back then Jack brought a gun, but didn't always pull it. Other times he had a knife. Most often he would just throttle a person with his bare hands or use anything that was within reach.

That day he had expected Tomás to just lift the window up and jump. As insane as it sounded, he'd seen many prefer to choose how they died than to face the unknown of being handed over to Gafino. Death was never the same for each person. For some, Gafino wanted their death to be drawn out. In those cases Jack would usually return them to Gafino. He preferred other methods.

What Jack had missed that day was what Tomás had done. He had taken PCP before he had opened the door to Jack. It wasn't that this made a person strong, it just prevented pain signals from reaching the brain. Which meant not only was he about to deal with a psychotic episode but he would come within an inch of having his life taken from him.

Tomás spun around and lunged at Jack. It was the one time Jack hadn't expected it. The knife came down hard into his shoulder. He winced in pain as he began a fight that lasted for over ten minutes. It was bloody and painful. By the time he had managed to pry the knife from his hand, and punch it up into Tomás's skull, the damage had already been done. His own stomach had been torn by the blade.

Jack's mind drifted back to the present. Upon reaching

the fourteenth floor he was mentally prepared for the worst. He wasn't planning on negotiating, or giving anyone a way out. Had he managed to get Jason to tell him more, he might have been able to ready himself, instead he remained empty-handed when the door opened.

# 14

Dana had been on edge ever since returning to the hotel that morning. What made it worse was that until Jack had texted her to let her know that he'd found Jason, all she could think about was the events that played out in Rockland Cove a year ago.

She wasn't prepared to go through it again.

This was the very reason why she didn't want to get involved with Jack again. Some people had baggage in their life. Past marriages, debt, kids, or personal issues. Jack took it all to a whole new level. She knew it was foolish to think he could walk away from a life in the mob. They didn't let them go easily, especially not those who had killed their own. There was a debt to be paid, and he was the one that now owed it.

A part of her wanted to call the police, but she thought that might only make it worse. Perhaps she would be considered an accessory to whatever shit he had been a part of since being in the city. What she wasn't aware of was that police already knew about her. And after losing sight of Jack, they were now en route to the hotel, as were two of the Sicilian Mafia. Both sides wanted her, for one reason only. To lure Jack back out into the open.

Anxious to hear word from Jack, Dana sat on the edge of the bed. The TV was on but the volume was down. She was biting her nails. It was a habit she had for years. Any time she was stressed out.

When she heard the banging at the door, she figured it was room service. Peering through the eyehole she saw two men.

"Police, open up."

"Show me your badges."

They flashed them.

After she unlocked the door, the men introduced themselves as Frank Banfield and Charlie Westwood. They asked if they could have a moment with her. She invited them in. The door to Jack's room was open.

She took a seat at the small table. Charlie looked around while Frank began questioning her.

"What is your association with Jack Winchester?"

"We date, or we have dated."

"You do or you don't?"

"It's complicated."

"I bet. Ms. Grant, what is the nature of your visit to the city?"

She shrugged. "New Year's Eve. We were planning on meeting his sister."

"Are you aware of Jack's affiliations with a crime family from New Jersey?"

And there it was. The question that was liable to send her down an endless stream of questions.

"No."

His eyebrows rose as he studied her. She always felt

uncomfortable in the presence of the police as if they were somehow trained to read minds. As absurd as it sounded that's what it felt like when she was around them. Charlie's phone buzzed, and he glanced at it.

"Frank, looks like we might have another shooting."

Frank nodded.

"Ms. Grant, we're going to take you down to the station."

"Am I under arrest?"

"No, but I'd like to have one of our officers get a bit more information from you."

"I'm waiting for my son."

"It shouldn't take too long."

She nodded reluctantly. She grabbed her coat and purse and exited the room. As they stepped outside into the hallway and began making their way down, two men came around the corner in the distance. Emotionless and without any regard for life, they pulled out handguns and fired. Before Frank could react, the first shot hit Charlie in the shoulder, sending him to the floor.

Frank grabbed a hold of Dana and pulled her back towards the room with one hand while the other raised his gun and began firing. But they couldn't get back into the room as Dana had left the keycard inside. Frank continued firing as the men strolled forward without a care in the world. Frank pushed Dana towards the stairwell. Once they got inside, he kept a hold of her while he fired shot after shot. Charlie was still out there. Frank tossed his phone to her. "Call the police now," he said.

"But..."

It seemed odd calling the police.

"I know."

The men forged forward even after they had pumped several more bullets into Charlie. His body went limp.

"Go." Frank yelled for Dana to get down the stairs. They raced to get down to the lobby. As they burst through the doors to the stairwell, Frank tried to tell people to get out but they must have thought he was joking. He raised his gun and let off a round. That was all it took. Guests in the lobby made a beeline for the doorway.

The sound of sirens could be heard in the distance. The two men came striding out with little fear. This was normal to them. There was no fear of who might see them, or even shoot at them. A security officer for the hotel pulled his weapon and fired a round before getting killed with a bullet to the head.

Frank had turned his head for just a few seconds. When he looked back, Dana was gone. She couldn't have gone out the main exit as people were fighting to get through the rotating door. Windows smashed as bullets snapped through the air. Frank had taken cover, hoping to hold them off until backup arrived. The two men had disappeared around a corner. He wasn't going to advance on them. He didn't even have a bulletproof vest on. It would have been pure suicide.

* * *

Dana had rushed down the hallway. It wasn't that she wanted to remain in the hotel. Everything inside of her was screaming to escape but one of the men was still following. Strangely though he wasn't firing at her. She had dashed back into the stairwell and was making her way up the stairs when she ran into the other. They had split up.

The next thing she sensed was the rumble of a vehicle. She could hear sirens but that was it. Light and darkness flashed in front of her. She thought she must be in the trunk of a car, or the box of a truck. She was cramped. Her head pounded with pain.

It was happening again.

All her fears had come to pass. She swore if she ever got out of this she would leave Jack behind. She loved him, but this was no life for a mother with a sixteen-year-old boy.

Jason. His face flashed in her mind. All she could do was hope he was okay. Where were they taking her? Why did they want her? She struggled to figure out where she was.

* * *

Back at the hotel the police arrived on scene. It was chaotic, but the gunfire had ended. For a while it was a tense situation. They had to call in SWAT as they had no way of knowing if the men were still in the building. Though Frank believed they were long gone by now. These were unlike anyone he had faced before. The look of resilience in their faces, they weren't going to stop until they got what they came for. Dana Grant.

He waited patiently outside until one of the SWAT team came out.

He shook his head. "No sign of her, sir."

"Okay." Frank nodded.

He watched medics bring out Charlie's body on a stretcher. He had worked with Charlie for over six years. He was a good man who didn't deserve to die that way. He had a family and a young child. Frank knew he would have to be the one to break the news to them. Announcing a death to anyone was tough. But to his partner's family. They would be utterly devastated.

One thing for sure, whoever did this would pay.

# 15

"Where the fuck is the money?" Spike yelled at Jack as he motioned for him to get inside. Jack used the first few seconds to count heads. In situations like this most would be overwhelmed. He couldn't count the number of times he had faced a loaded gun, or been outnumbered. He'd learned to push down panic. Panic could get you killed. It made you freeze. You became a victim of your circumstances. That wasn't him. He listened to what was being said, but his mind was thinking about the number of people in the room, distance, timing, weapons, and cover. He saw Jason and could tell he was scared. Beyond him were four other men, he could hear even more, but they were out of sight.

"Are you listening? Where is the money?"

"It's in the car."

Spike pressed the gun against Jack's head. One slip and it would be over.

"Why didn't you bring it in?"

"And take the risk of losing your money?"

"Tyrone, Jamal, take this fool down to get the green."

Two large guys came over. Both of them were dressed as if they had just stepped off the basketball court. Both were packing heat. There was no telling how fast either of them was.

"The boy," Jack said.

"He stays here until you return," Spike replied.

Jack nodded and was quickly shoved out into the hallway by both men. Every step he took as they descended to the ground floor he was thinking about disarming them. There was no clean way of doing this. He would have to take rapid action. He turned slightly and felt a shove.

"Eyes ahead," one of them said behind him.

Casually, Jack reached a hand into his jacket twisted the gun around. Without even taking it out of the holster, he proceeded to fire off a round through the jacket. The bullet hit one man in the leg. He dropped. Without missing a beat, Jack spun around and was about to unload on the next guy but he was already on top of him. They fell backwards and toppled down a few remaining steps. Pain shot through his back as the hard edges slammed into his ribs. He was now wrestling with the gun and trying to prevent it going off. Two rounds fired, barely missing him. A third went off and it skimmed his shoulder, causing him to wince in pain. Finally, he turned it back on the guy and fired four rounds into his chest. He lay there for a moment to catch his breath before he ascended the steps. It was in moments like this that his mind became highly focused. Whether it was because adrenaline was pumping fast through his body or just out of habit, he would get tunnel vision.

A minute later he was back up the stairs. He plowed his foot into the door twice before it burst open and he came face to face with two men beyond the threshold. He had grabbed up one of the men's handguns. That's when he started firing. The key was to keep moving forward. He hit one of the men in the gut and the other in the knee. They screamed and slid around on the floor.

Jack rushed in, scooping up their weapons. One of them raised his hand, and a bullet ripped through his fingers. He wasn't concerned about killing them. They were in too much pain to be able to be of any further threat.

Five minutes later he was staring down at numerous dead bodies around him. The few who were still alive were writhing around on the floor in agony. Jason stared as if shock had set in. His face was pale.

"Let's go."

Jason had no reason to argue. They were out the door and were going down the stairs when they saw men coming up. There had to have been at least ten of them. Voices echoed. He turned around and pushed Jason into a hallway full of doors. They had already come down five floors. They went along banging on doors in the hopes that someone would let them in. It wasn't like they could go to the roof. The apartment block was not attached to any other buildings. No one would open the doors. Then Jack spotted a door cracked open. The man inside saw that Jack had spotted him and slammed it.

"Please let us in."

"Go away, you'll get us killed."

As he was banging another door opened beside them.

"Quick. In here."

An African American man let them inside. He slammed it closed. Jason bent over, gripping his knees, trying desperately to catch his breath.

"Thank you," Jack said.

There was only one way out and that was down.

"I don't know what you've done and I don't want

to know. As soon as the coast is clear, you are to leave. You understand?"

Jack nodded.

# 16

Frank was getting reamed out by his boss for what had gone down. They had more casualties than they had anticipated. The two unknown men had not only killed Charlie, but taken out a security guard and three civilians.

Another officer came into the room just as the conversation between the two of them was starting to get heated.

He handed the boss a folder and then quickly exited. The blinds on the office door had been pulled to prevent prying eyes. Not that it was of much use as the yelling could probably have been heard two floors below.

Daniel Bomer had been Frank's boss for more years than he could count. He was the kind of man that would move mountains if it meant catching his guy, but you didn't want to get on the bad side of him. He'd brought grown men to tears in his office.

"Dominick Morello and Anthony Lombardo." He tossed two photos that had been taken from the hotel's surveillance camera. You want to tell me why we have two of the Sicilian Mafia in our city?"

Frank handed back the photos.

"It has to be related to Jack Winchester."

"Right. The guy you so happened to let go."

"We didn't have anything on him."

"We had enough to keep him for twenty-four hours. That might have given us more. Now he's gone, we have two potential kidnappings on our hands and two shooters on the loose. Do you know how this is going to look? The amount of crap I'm going to have to explain? Our phone lines are already tied up with the media hounding us at every turn."

That was all he cared about. How this was going to look. How it might affect his reputation.

"We'll find him."

"You better." He let out a long breath. "Have you spoken to Charlie's family yet?"

Frank shook his head.

"Well, get on that. I don't want them to hear about his death from the news."

He took a swig of his coffee and gathered together the papers on his desk.

"And Jack Winchester?"

"What is the deal with you and him?

He rocked back in his chair tapping his pencil against the table.

"I knew him as a kid, that's it."

"Find him before these guys do."

When Frank left the office, he stopped by his desk to grab a bottle of headache tablets. He tossed two back and washed it down with a cone of water.

"Hey Banfield, see you fucked up another job."

"Fuck you, Randall."

There was always an air of competition in the

department. Everyone was trying to one up each other and land a promotion. Frank didn't want to get promoted. Hell, he would have been glad to be demoted. At least then he wouldn't get his ear chewed out every other week.

It seemed like forever since he was an officer patrolling the streets and up to his neck in paperwork. He would hear many of the officers complaining. Saying how they wanted to get out of uniform, become a detective. If he knew the type of shit he had to deal with, they wouldn't have even put in for the position.

* * *

After returning home to get some well-deserved sleep that evening, he tried to get comfortable. Sleep, he thought. It just seemed foreign. He'd be lucky if he got one or two hours before he would be called back out.

He switched on some music. It was Bach. There was nothing that soothed his mind more than the sound of piano playing lightly. It pushed out the noise in his head. The sound of the streets. The memories of seeing one too many deaths. Most got into the police to make a difference, but that was just foolish in hindsight. You didn't change anything in this world.

You merely put away one criminal, and another popped up in their place. It was a never-ending cycle that he only wished he could escape. In many ways he could see the appeal of the work Jack did, or at least he had done. The past year had been quiet. Since Gafino was gone, there had been a slump in criminal activity, at least the kind he dealt with. Domestics, traffic, and hate crimes made up the majority of calls for officers. Homicides were usually cleared up fast. At least the ones that weren't committed by a member of a crime family.

He'd grown used to waking early and returning home late. He would look over case files and try to piece together who was responsible.

Frank lived alone. He'd been married just over three years to Lillian Routhaby. She soon grew tired of sleeping alone. He couldn't fault her. She was a good woman. He'd met her through an art gallery that he would frequent when he had some downtime. At first she had been very accepting of his work. The calls he would get in the early hours that would pull him away. The nights he wouldn't speak because he had seen horrors that no person should ever have to witness. The city held secrets behind locked doors. Evil permeated every facet of society. Young or old, rich or poor, he had seen all of them affected, and each one commit atrocities.

It took its toll on a person. A marriage was hard to sustain in his line of work. The department saw more divorces than most other careers. Of course he always imagined he would be different; the one that slipped through the cracks unscathed.

Frank poured himself two fingers of scotch and took a seat in his leather chair. He felt the golden liquid burn as he allowed the music to lull him into a deep slumber.

# 17

Jack was getting no response from Dana. They had been holed up inside this apartment for well over six hours. They had heard the banging on the doors as men went room to room asking if anyone had seen anything.

But thankfully no one had seen Dwayne let them in.

They'd learned a little about the man in the apartment. He lived alone. Ex-military. He'd done eleven years in the Marine Corps. Nothing bothered him more than coming back to a country that seemed to abandon its veterans. He walked with a limp, something they came to discover was a prosthetic leg. He'd been shot in Afghanistan. They weren't able to save the limb.

"You ever married, Dwayne?"

"Nope. No one would put up with my shit and I wouldn't put up with theirs."

Jack chuckled.

"You know about these men running this building?" Jack asked.

"They moved in four years ago. Took over the whole damn place. They walk around as though the world owes them a living. But nobody owes anyone anything. I got no handouts. Hell, I was lucky to get a prosthetic leg. And I'm pretty damn sure they are taking payment out somewhere else."

Jack checked how many rounds he had left. He had one magazine in his pocket, and about five bullets in each gun.

"You never thought about moving out of here? Getting an apartment in a safer neighborhood?"

"Why the fuck should I? I grew up here. These assholes should have left a long time ago. You did us a favor."

Jack glanced up at him. Both Jack and Jason were crouched down on the floor trying to listen for anyone coming while Dwayne shuffled around the kitchen. He brought two plates. On each was a sandwich with bologna in the middle.

"It's not much. But…"

"Thank you."

The two of them scarfed it down. For all they knew it could be their last meal. Jack could have sworn he'd seen one of the men coming up carrying an AK-47. His first priority right now was getting them out of here alive and finding out what had happened to Dana. As soon as he got back to the hotel, he would send them both back to Rockland Cove. After that, he planned on showing up at Leo Carlone's restaurant. Even if it meant his own life being taken, he wouldn't have any harm come to his sister.

Not long after the men had been performing their search another group showed up to a chorus of sirens. The police crawled all over the place. They didn't stay long though. They knew better than to linger around one of the most dangerous and roughest parts of Brooklyn. Crime had swept through here and taken over. Young kids were armed and wouldn't think twice about blasting you in the chest with a shotgun if it meant they got more money and advancement in their gang.

"Do you see many people show up here?"

"Like who?" Dwayne asked.

"The kind of men who don't look like they fit in?"

"Yeah, twice a month. Like clockwork. A black SUV pulls up outside, a bag is handed off to them, and they leave. I never see them get out. But I did get a license plate." He scratched his head. "Now where did I put that?"

He shuffled around the table. His hands rooted around in a pile of papers. Dwayne's apartment looked as if it hadn't been cleaned in years. Piles of old papers stacked high, books, and military gear were sprawled all over the place. He didn't look as if he cooked for himself as he didn't even have a stove. Just a microwave. No doubt it was frozen dinners every night.

Dwayne found it and handed it over to Jack. Jack gave it back after memorizing it.

"Well, let's see if the coast is clear," Jack said.

Jack got up and peered out the peephole. There was no one there. He cracked the door ever so slightly and listened.

"You ready, kid?"

Jason nodded.

"Thank you, Dwayne."

"No need to thank me. You did me a favor. Those punks got what was coming to them. By the way, exit through the laundry area. There is a door that leads out to the pool."

Jack's lip curled up. Dwayne was someone who understood that sometimes you had to fight. There was no other choice. What he didn't know was how real that would become later.

Jason and Jack scurried down the hallway, raced down the stairs, and ducked into the laundry room. Within two minutes they were outside. They passed what looked like a pool. It was empty, full of garbage, and had an overturned shopping cart inside it. Jack snorted as he passed a sign that read, Paradise Apartments.

# 18

Dana wasn't sure how long she had been in the trunk of the car, only that she had passed out again. When she awoke, she found herself lying on a concrete floor. It was cold. She blinked hard. She felt nauseated. She hauled herself into an upright position. The skin around her wrists ached as did her ankles. They had bound her legs and wrists with rope.

The first thing she saw was bottles of wine. Rows and rows of wine covered in dust. She was in a wine cellar. As she turned to her right, she jerked her head back, surprised to see another woman. She was younger than Dana. In her early thirties. She squinted as if trying to recall where she had seen her face. A momentary brain relapse, then she remembered a photo. It was Milly, Jack's sister.

"Milly?"

Milly had her eyes closed, she opened them and looked at Dana. Milly looked as if someone had given her a beating. Her face was bloodied and partly swollen around the right eye.

"How do you know me?" she said in an almost inaudible voice.

"Your brother, Jack. We were coming to see you."

"Dana?"

She nodded. Milly burst into tears.

"It's okay. It's okay. Jack will get us out of this."

She had no way of knowing if he even knew where they were.

* * *

Across the city Jack was still no wiser to what had happened to Dana. His thoughts were of his sister's safety. The more he mulled over what they had done, the more he felt rage swelling inside of him. He and Jason had found the nearest hotel and ordered a taxi. As they sat, waiting for it to arrive, Jack thought about the events that had put his sister in the treatment center.

At one time she had been carefree. Both of them were until his father would get drunk. The beatings came frequently. When they did, he would protect his sister by having her hide in the closet, under the bed, or out in the yard. He did anything to prevent his father turning his attention on her. The abuse she suffered at the hands of that man wasn't just physical, it was sexual.

It had only got worse when his stepmother had shown up. She seemed to focus her rage on Milly more than Jack. It was if she felt threatened by another female in the house. Jack believed it was a combination of things that led up to the death of his father. Once Eddie caught wind of what was happening to Milly after the last beating Jack received, that was the tipping point. Some said Eddie had beaten him with his bare hands there in the home. But Jack knew that wasn't Eddie's way. He wasn't into torture. He would have acted swiftly. Taking him out with a bullet and then disposing of his body. The body later found in the Hudson River.

After his death, Eddie had taken in Milly but the trauma had been too much. She couldn't function. She would go into herself and stare at the wall for hours. Eddie had made the decision to put her into treatment. Jack couldn't blame him. It was hard enough trying to cope with his own responsibilities but with Milly it was too much.

There was a five-year gap between the two of them. Jack was eighteen by the time he was begun working for Gafino full-time. But he was sixteen when he moved in with Eddie.

He and Eddie would take turns visiting her, hoping that she would one day snap out of the dazed state. The doctors said it could take months. It took years.

Jack let out a long breath as they got out of the taxi. When he arrived there were no police cars outside the hotel, but there were two news vans. A small crowd had gathered. The place was taped off. He saw gun holes in the window. The glass had split and shattered in some areas.

"Sorry, sir, you can't go in there," a security guard stepped forward.

"But I'm booked here," Jack replied.

"What's your room number?"

Jack gave it and the security guard went inside and spoke to the woman at the front desk. She glanced up and looked at them outside. She picked up a phone. Everything about it made him feel uneasy. While she was doing that, the security officer came outside.

He motioned for them to follow. "Sir, please, come this way."

"Why?" Jack asked.

"It will all be explained. I just need you to come with me."

"No, I'd prefer to wait here."

"That wasn't a request," the security guard replied.

Jack knew where this was heading. In that instant he saw a uniformed officer appear inside the lobby. He immediately spun around and pushed Jason in the opposite direction.

"Run."

The security guard caught a hold of Jack. Jack jammed the palm of his hand up into his nose, crushing it. The guard dropped to his knees. Blood went everywhere. Jack turned and bolted. People were pointing, others yelling.

"What the hell's going on?" Jason yelled as he charged across the road. Jack dodged traffic as cars swerved erratically to avoid hitting him. Another security guard tried to chase them down. They lost him in the surge of people filling up the streets. Once they knew they were clear, they ducked into a Chinese restaurant to catch their breath.

"Come. You eat."

A Chinese man motioned for them to take a seat. Jack waved him off, and they left the building. Back out on the streets it was getting even busier. The stores and streets were lit up like a Christmas tree.

"Jack, what about my mother?" Jason asked, looking distraught.

As much as Jack didn't want to be running from the police he had little choice. He knew, as well as any other crime family member, that Leo Carlone had informers who were police officers. They were on payroll. Who they were was anyone's guess. Right now he needed answers. And there was only one person that would be willing to give them.

They moved through the crowd and ducked into a retail clothing store. Jack tossed the guy some money, and they grabbed different jackets. They even bought New Year's hats. They were blue and looked like a top hat. Everyone was wearing them. Right now they needed to blend in. Not that police would be able to find them very well in a city this large. But by now they would have put the word out to officers patrolling the streets.

Horns were honking, and cars were bumper to bumper as they navigated their way around the wet and cold streets. Jack pulled out the card that Frank had given him when they had released him. There was a phone number on the front. That was his official extension at the department. But scribbled on the back was his home number and address.

There was only one reason he would give him that. He wanted Jack to know that he could trust him. That whatever his involvement had been in the murder of Eddie Carmine, and the abduction of his sister, he could reach out to someone he knew. Jack knew it was a ploy; a means to gain his trust. In fact, he'd considered tossing it earlier. He was glad he'd kept it now.

Frank was no longer living in New Jersey. He had an apartment in Brooklyn. His home was located in Windsor Terrace. It was close to Greenwood Cemetery. They hopped on the F subway line and arrived in a small but quiet tree-lined neighborhood. Rows of brick houses mixed with wood frame houses that had been built in the early 1900s.

"You think he'll be in?" Jason asked.

"If he's not, we'll wait."

It took them another ten minutes from the subway station to reach his home. Jack wasn't taking any chances. They snuck around the side and tried the back door. It was locked. He shook the windows a little until he found one that was unlocked. Sliding it up he helped Jason through and then followed.

It was a swanky place, with Victorian décor yet made to look modern. An elegant interior with arched doorways. A warm yellow glow seeped in from under the door. They were in what looked like a study. Jack looked around. Books to do with criminology lined the table. Everything was well organized and pristine in appearance. Jack cracked the door open to find Frank asleep in a chair. A light music was playing. He moved over to the player and turned it off. Frank stirred.

"Hello?" Frank gazed out from beneath heavy lids.

Jack turned around.

"Hey, Frank," Jack replied quietly.

Frank's eyes darted between him and Jason.

"What are you doing here?"

Jack let out a long breath. "I need answers."

"Jack, you need to turn yourself in. They've got her."

"Dana?" he asked.

"Who else?"

"They've got my mother? Who has?" Jason began to look panicked.

"The Sicilian Mafia. You've pissed off the wrong people this time."

"How do you know?" Jack asked.

"I saw them. Surveillance."

"What do we do?" Jason asked.

Jack didn't say anything.

"Jack?" Jason asked again.

"Just give me a minute to think."

"This is about Gafino, isn't it?" Frank asked.

In all the time he'd worked with Gafino he had only met the Sicilian Mafia twice. On both occasions they seemed like any other crime family. But what he had heard of them was brutal. Their methods for payback were never just a bullet in the head. They took things to a whole new level of sick. They made Gafino's work look like kiddy play.

"You want a drink?" Frank asked.

Jack's eyes shifted to Frank. He nodded.

"A drink?" Jason looked perplexed. "We need to get my mother back."

"And we will. Take a seat," Jack said.

Jack wasn't in the mood for baby-sitting. His mind was running a mile a minute. He envisioned the worst. He tried to make sense of what their end game was. They always had one. Sometimes it was money. Mostly, it was revenge. Nothing more.

"Do you think they'll kill them?" Jason asked.

"No. They want me. Then, they might."

Jason slumped down in a chair, his hands over his face.

"This is all my fault. I shouldn't have gone to see that guy. I shouldn't have even come along. If it had just been you two, you wouldn't have come looking for me."

"Jason, don't. What's done is done."

Frank handed Jack a drink. He downed it in one go. It did little to alleviate the anxiety he was feeling. He had no game plan. No sense of how to approach this other than using pure violence.

"Let us help. Give up the details on Gafino," Frank said.

"I'm not going back to Rikers, Frank."

"Either way you lose here, Jack. You go in there guns blazing, you are not only liable to get yourself killed, but even if you do make it out, they are going to put you inside and toss the key away."

"I just need time to think this through."

"There is no time," Frank replied.

A few minutes passed. Jack stared into the fire. He chuckled as he heard the sound of sirens in the distance. Frank had made the call when he went to pour him a drink.

"Take care of the kid," Jack said.

"Jack?"

"Jack, you can't leave me here," Jason said.

"No, you need to stay with him."

"But my mother."

"Frank," Jack said as he got up.

Frank nodded. As the sirens got louder, Jack went to the back door, unlocked it. He cast a final glance over his shoulder at Jason and then disappeared into the night.

Calling it in was what Frank had to do. Giving him time to get away, that was Frank still being a friend. Even as he scaled over fences and made his way out of the neighborhood, he could still hear the sound of police sirens in the distance. It had been a long while since he had run from the police. While he was only thirty-nine, he was getting too old for this shit. He couldn't believe it had come to this. Every action, every decision he'd made had led him to this very point now.

He'd wanted to leave behind the past. To put it all behind him. But it wasn't that easy. The past didn't want to let him go. It wouldn't until he finished what he had started. He reached into his pocket and pulled out the key to Eddie Carmine's storage locker.

Jack heard a chopper overhead. They were looking for him. It was close to eleven o'clock. The night was at its blackest. By the time he made it to the storage facility located on the west side of Brooklyn, hardly any stars were out.

Brooklyn Storage Facility was open twenty-four hours. A line of concrete garages with orange doors trailed off into the distance. He wandered up the seemingly endless number of lockers until he found 412. He unlocked it and pulled up the metal door. It clanged and echoed into the night. He reached for a cord to turn the light on. Once light flooded the room, he pulled the door down behind him.

He rubbed his hands together. It was getting colder.

Gazing around at what Eddie had stored, his eyes widened. He had an entire arsenal of weapons, a computer, and unknown boxes. He pulled them out and one by one started going through them. Some of them were just filled with everyday belongings. Memorabilia, clothes, photos, and military medals. Eddie had never been one for storing medals in fancy frames. In his eyes, the war was never over. He wouldn't sleep at night.

Jack pulled out a long case and opened it. Inside was an AR-15 assault rifle. He wasn't planning on taking it. It would create too much noise. Swat would be called in. As much as he could have used it, he laid it to one side for the time being. In another silver container the size of a briefcase he found two handguns. Each case held two 9mm Glocks with laser guide rods. Each one held fifteen bullets. There was also extra ammo, more than enough. Inside another container was a bulletproof vest, flash bangs, and grenades. Hell, Eddie must have stolen all of this from his days in the military or he'd become an avid collector.

It was hard to imagine why he would have kept all of this. Inside another box was a stack of cash. There had to have been over twenty grand. Why would he have kept that here? He wasn't exactly living in the Ritz. If he was doing well financially why didn't he live in the lap of luxury?

Inside another smaller container, he found an envelope. It was addressed to Jack in Rockland Cove.

# 19

Jack tore the edge of the envelope and removed the letter inside. A pair of keys dropped out. He sat down on an overturned bucket and began reading.

*Jack,*

*If you're reading this now, I'm no longer here. I've written this letter so many times. I've tried to mail it even more times.*

*It's funny the path we take in life. The older I have got the more I've realized that so much of what we do is meaningless. When we are young, we throw ourselves into all manner of things. We think we are invincible and that nothing will touch us. Perhaps that's why I joined the military. Maybe that's why many others do. There is a driving need to feel a sense of purpose, direction, and meaning in our lives. And what better way than to align ourselves with a group who say they are trying to change the world. To make it a better place. But truth is, it's all the same. There is no good or bad side. Each of us makes choices that we justify as being right.*

*Every side thinks they are good. The rest is just hearsay.*

*When I met your mother, she was the most beautiful person I had laid eyes on. She had a warm heart. Somehow she could see into my core. She saw the pain I hid. The mask that I wore to keep people at a distance.*

*When I joined the military, I knew things between us wouldn't stay the same. I blame myself in many ways for the breakdown of our relationship. And I would like to say your mother was better off without me in her life. But that wouldn't be true. I never imagined what would happen to her, or either of you.*

*After a few months in the service for Uncle Sam, I learned your mother was pregnant with you. She told me you were my son, but I didn't believe it.*

Jack stopped reading. It felt as if someone had sucker punched him. He'd heard the rumors that Eddie was his father. But he was never quite sure. When you grow up in a household, especially the one he did, you didn't question. You accepted the hand you had been dealt. He continued reading…

*By the time I got out, she had already been living for years with the one you believed to be your father. From what I know, he is the father of Milly, but you are my son. I've come to believe that.*

*Jack, what I did that night when I murdered the man you believed was your father, was for you, your sister, and your mother. I'm sorry I wasn't there from the time you were born, to protect you and keep you from harm. I tried to persuade you not to get involved with Gafino. But you are like me in so many ways. Stubborn, driven, and will only learn after the fact.*

*But now, I want you to know about me. I didn't work at the factory. I did for a time. But I earned my money doing other work. Work that helped people. Those who were looked over by the court system. Those who deserved protection, justice, and someone to be in their corner. There should be enough money stashed here to help you if you need it. And if you wish to continue the work that I began, you'll find out everything you need to know on the computer. It's not easy, Jack. But you and I are cut from the same cloth. Gafino would have said we are killers. But that's not true. Killing is easy. Anyone can do that. What determines who we are is our choices. You have a choice, Jack. I know you are haunted by what you have done. The bloodshed. The lives you have taken. And maybe you wish you could reverse time. I wish I could. But what you can do is determine how you finish. How? By helping others. Those who are tread upon by unscrupulous individuals.*

*But you must know this. It's not an easy path to take. You can't surround yourself with those who might be harmed. I think you already know that. Maybe you won't have someone there beside you at the end of the day. But when you rest your head on that pillow, you will know that you have done what others wouldn't do. You will have helped those who couldn't help themselves.*

*I can't make that choice for you. And I would understand if you chose to walk from everything and lead a quiet life.*

*But I think you will know what to do when you are ready.*

*You will find the set of keys belongs to a truck that I bought a year ago. Ownership is in your name. It's not much, and I never learned to drive but it's for you. You'll find it on the premises. I've paid to have it stored in one of the larger units. Use the second key to get in.*

*For now, all I can say is what I should have said, years ago.*

*I love you, son.*

*Eddie*

Jack felt himself becoming choked up. He paused for a moment to pull himself together. Inside the envelope was one more thing. A photo, he pulled it out. It was old, yellowed by time. A younger Eddie Carmine stood holding a child, with Jack's mother beside him. On the back was a date, and the names. Wendy, Eddie, and Jack.

He placed the letter and photo back into the envelope and pocketed it. He checked both Glocks, racked the slide, and then tucked both behind him near the small of his back. He would return later to look everything over. For now, his main priority was the safety of his sister and Dana. Outside he could hear the sound of sirens in the distance. He knew it wouldn't be easy; police would be combing the streets looking for him.

He exited the storage unit and went and searched for locker number forty-six. It was on the far side of the property. He unlocked the door and slid it up. Inside was a black Ford truck. It wasn't brand-new, but it was in good condition.

# 20

Leo Carlone could feel another panic attack coming on. He had a lot to lose. His wife and daughter were the most important to him. His livelihood came next. At one time he would have said his reputation mattered. But that was when he was young. Now that was just a joke. Clinging to that was the reason Gafino was buried.

No, now with two women being held in his wine cellar, things were getting way out of control. After Gafino and most of his crew had been wiped out by Jack, he had spent the first month worrying that he would be next. He'd watched Jack rise through the ranks. He was the perfect foot solider. The man they sent in to do the dirty work. If they were the military, he was like special ops. The guy had a knack for taking people out. He rarely made mistakes. That's why when they learned of his incarceration, they were stunned.

He wanted Jack dead for numerous reasons. His son's death was only one of them, but he was scared himself. There were few people that really made him sweat. Jack was one of them.

Of course there were others like Jack. Those who did the hits for the older guys. But none of them had the finesse or aptitude to keep them out of the crosshairs. So most wound up dead.

Gafino had a sure thing. Everyone knew it. There were ten of them. The older generation had all but cashed in their chips and were now enjoying the good life in the Caribbean. The few that hadn't got out, were stuck in New York still working the same game. Extortion was the lifeblood of their work.

Leo had been the only one that had tried to think about the end game. He wanted to get out of the extortion business. He was closing in on sixty years of age.

He wanted to live long enough to see his grandchildren.

Having Jack coming after him was the last thing he wanted.

Three months after the death of Gafino he had sent men up to Rockland Cove. He had got wind of where his son had been murdered and assumed that was where Jack would be. His guys spent a weekend searching for him and came up empty-handed.

They didn't have the manpower or time to dick around searching for him. It was meant to be an easy kill. A shot from a distance. Keep it clean, he said. It never occurred.

The goal was to kill him before he killed them. Though after three months had passed, they had ruled out that this was anything more than payback for Gafino. As much as he missed his son, he wasn't going to get his hands dirty or finish his life chewing on the end of a gun barrel. He knew if he kept digging and searching for Jack, he would eventually show up.

A month after that, Jack was the least of his

concerns. The Sicilian Mafia were. They had a long partnership with them. Drugs were made down in South America, exported to Italy, and then shipped into different ports along the East Coast. It had worked for years. The feds spent more time searching the border between the USA and Mexico than they did some offbeat towns in New England.

Only Gafino knew the towns that shipments were coming in from. He had the dates and times of when product would show up. The problem was, if there was no one there to collect, it was usually destroyed. They couldn't return with it. This meant the Sicilian Mafia was taking a huge hit in the pocket. With Gafino out of the loop, business on the streets had taken a nosedive. Other crime families were moving in and it wouldn't be long before everything they had established over the years would be gone.

But getting that sorted out wasn't first on his priority list. Vito from the Sicilian Mafia wanted to be paid. None of the old-timers had the money. Most had taken that long overdue vacation when they learned of Gafino's hit. Now all that remained was a handful of men and an extortion business that could never pull in enough money to cover the loss that Vito had suffered.

The only way to get back to business was to take out Jack. He knew it might kill him. That Jack might end his life, but it was the only way he could see them moving forward. To hold off the inevitable. It meant pulling strings. Making dangerous decisions like taking his sister. Anything to lure Jack back out into the open.

To make him face off against the Sicilian Mafia. As there was no way Leo was going to be able to come up with the money they wanted. A quick twist and choice of words and they bought it. They saw that Jack was the one to blame. And in many ways he was. That was not a lie. What Leo had kept from Vito was that he had hoped Jack would kill them and spare him once he returned his sister. He would claim he was forced into it. That he had no control or say in the matter. He would appeal to Jack's better side. If he even had one? That was debatable.

He had heard from Roy when he was alive that Jack had another side to him. That beyond the brutal acts he committed, there was a side that wanted normality. Whatever normal was. In their world normal was making others do what you wanted them to. Normal was being on top and making sure your enemies were below you. Making sure they knew the pecking order.

He had some of his men bring the two women food and water. He wanted to treat them well. Give them a sense that at least he was on their side. That he wasn't behind all of this. Then when the time came and Jack showed up, as Leo fully believed he would, they would speak for him. It was a slim shot. But the only one he had. It was that, or die at the hands of Vito.

Leo had arranged to have his wife and daughter take a vacation to California for a month. His wife's family lived out there. It would give Vito long enough to deal with this matter. It would also give Leo peace of mind that they were out of harm's way.

Vito was in the middle of chewing out Dominick

and Anthony. The news was playing in the background. Reports on a large shooting that had taken place at a hotel in Brooklyn.

"This is all we need. I told you to be discreet about it."

"There was police already on site. What do you expect is going to happen? We got her, didn't we?" Dominick replied.

Vito was as tall as the other two. All three of them looked like prizefighters. They weren't your stereotypical overweight Italian mobsters. They resembled MMA fighters.

"You shot a cop. You know how much heat that is going to bring down on us?" Vito said.

"We have them," Dominick replied.

"You have no one. We need Jack. Not these bitches."

"He'll show up," Leo added, stepping out of the shadows at the back of the room. "Just be prepared."

Vito laughed. "There you go again, making out this

guy is some sort of machine. He's human. He bleeds."

"Yes. Just not like us."

Vito shook his head.

"Probably best we move this to a different location. I've got a house on Long Island," Leo said.

"And, how do you expect him to know where you are?"

"We'll have one of the women phone. That way he knows they're alive."

"And you really think he is just going to turn himself over?"

"He will if he's given the option of them being let go."

"I thought you wanted revenge?"

"I want him dead. Not the women. I'm not an animal."

Vito laughed. "That's why I like you, Leo, you really believe your hands aren't stained in blood. Alright, we do it your way."

Vito nodded to Dominick. He went off to collect

Dana.

A few minutes later he emerged. Dana was struggling. Vito handed her a phone.

"Phone Jack."

"I don't—"

He didn't even let her finish before he backhanded her in the face. Her cheek became instantly red.

"Do it. And on speakerphone."

Dana took hold of the phone and made a call. It rang a few times then Jack picked up.

"Jack."

"Dana?"

"Heard a lot about you, Jack. Do you know me?" Vito said.

"Yeah, you're the asshole I'm going to kill."

Vito let out a chuckle. "I like this guy." He paused. "Listen up. This is pretty simple. You now know what we will do. If you want to see your sister and this bitch again, come out to…" Vito looked at Leo for the address. Leo didn't say it. He wrote it down on a piece of paper. He didn't want Jack to think that he had anything to do with this.

"You got it?"

"I'm coming for you," Jack said.

"Good, I look forward to meeting you."

# 21

Jack was already on his way to Leo Carlone's restaurant when the call came in. They had wanted to wait until the next morning for the meeting. He knew this was all going to be a setup. They would leave in the night. They had no intentions of letting go of his sister or Dana. It was all about power. Control and showing others what would happen if you crossed them. Jack had seen it all in his time working for Gafino. The Sicilian Mafia were no different. They were brutal but they made the same mistakes that others did. They allowed their pride to get in the way. It prevented them from thinking clearly. They would make snap decisions. Wing it. And still believe they would come out on top. That was why Gafino was dead. He really thought he was an untouchable. He believed his own press. That was his first mistake. His second was being too greedy, and his third was double-crossing Jack.

It didn't take him long to reach the restaurant. He parked across the street. Way out of sight. The truck's windows were tinted and there were still so many people on the streets celebrating the New Year. He saw a large crowd of college kids pass by; they were hooting and hollering, completely drunk out of their minds. Vehicles passed by blasting out music. The bass reverberated enough that he could feel it in his own vehicle. He slumped down in his seat looking across at the men coming out of the building. He spotted his sister and Dana. The men manhandled them into a black SUV while Leo and four of his men got into another car.

As they pulled out, he followed, making sure to keep two other vehicles between them. The journey out to Lindenhurst, Long Island, would take just over forty minutes. Lindenhurst was east of the infamous Amityville.

He was familiar with the location of Leo's home. He hadn't changed it in all the time he'd known him. It was their coastal retreat. It had fourteen rooms, four bathrooms, a pool, and a tennis court. What he remembered about the place was everything was white inside, except the floors, which were made from dark hardwood. White walls, white sofa and chairs, white tables. It was something to see. It backed out onto the coast. It had its own private beach. Leo used to always go on about how he didn't have money, but that place had to be worth a bundle.

Jack rubbed his eyes trying to keep awake. He was mentally exhausted by everything that had taken place since they'd arrived in New York. The continual battle to leave behind his past had taken its toll. He thought about Eddie's letter on the way over. It was strange to think about him as his father. In his mind he was just a close friend. And what was on the computer? What was he talking about? Helping people? He had always thought that Eddie had worked at the auto dealers but by the looks of the guns and money inside the storage area; he was beginning to wonder what else he didn't know about him.

Once they arrived at Leo's, Jack watched them pull into the driveway and disappear behind the evergreen bushes. He parked across the road and jumped out. He was dressed in a black leather jacket, dark jeans, and shoes. It wasn't exactly the most comfortable gear to be wearing. Especially when he was about to go into the lion's den. But it would have to do.

He reached into the back of the truck and took out the case that contained the assault rifle. He had taken it just in case. He didn't like using weapons with such firepower. They attracted too much attention, but in this case he thought it actually might be helpful. He thought about having the police show up.

They had told him they had the women. He saw them. He could just call the police and let them handle it. They would raid the home and more than likely get them out. The men inside would be too busy focusing on trying to escape to think about taking the women with them. Besides, they already had two of them on surveillance shooting up the hotel.

But then what if they escaped? What if they got hauled in? He knew Leo had ties with the police. A few phone calls and he could be out on bail. And as for the Sicilian Mafia, they could get out. It wasn't a far stretch to see it happen.

As much as he didn't like going it alone, he had little choice. The only thing that was motivating him at this point was the rage he felt for them killing Eddie. At least if Jack died in a shootout with these men, it would finally be over. He would no longer have to struggle. No longer have to face the demons in his head. The ones that constantly reminded him of the murders he had committed as a mobster.

Jack cast a glance down the street, took the assault rifle out of the case. That's when he noticed a suppressor. He chuckled, grabbed it up and tossed the rifle over his shoulder by the strap. He did one last check on his ammo and then raced across the road. He would approach the house from the rear. He had remembered that the back portion of the house had large windows. It would give him a good sense of what he was up against. Where people were positioned. He fully expected some of Leo's men to be out patrolling the grounds. They weren't stupid. They would be waiting for him to show his face. No doubt, they had been given instructions to shoot on sight.

He crouched down, keeping close to the trees. Snow covered every inch of the property. It was starting to come down heavily. He spotted two of Leo's men in the rear. They were talking to each other. One of them lit a cigarette, and then they parted ways to perform a routine check. He pressed his back against a tree and looked off into the distance as one of the men flashed a light into the tree line. He held his breath with his hand on the trigger as he saw it sweep past him. He heard the man's footsteps move past him.

Slowly he moved forward with purpose. He would

take each of them out, one by one. Using bullets only when needed.

He crept through the snow behind the man who was holding nothing more than a handgun. Jack surveyed the area. The man stopped for a second and he thought that he had heard him. But he must have relit a cigarette. Jack took advantage of that momentary distraction. He came up behind, in one fluid motion he smothered the man's mouth with his hand. His other arm went around him to prevent him from going for his gun. A quick twist and he snapped the guy's neck. The body went limp. He dragged him back into the tree line, removed his handgun, and kicked snow over his body. Again he waited until the other man appeared at the back of the house.

"Joe?" the man called out before sweeping his flashlight like a lighthouse. Jack remained as still as a statue. As it passed by, he pulled his assault rifle around and screwed on the suppressor. The man was still searching for his partner when the bullet hit him. It was followed by another and then he dropped. Jack scrambled across the yard. His mind was firing on all cylinders. He knew there were at least another two or three that might be walking the perimeter. He dragged the body into a shed and covered it with a tarp. The last thing he needed right now was to have an alarm sounding.

From where he stood he had a good view of the living area. It was lit up in a yellow glow. If he was after one person, he could have shot them from outside. The thought had crossed his mind. He probably could take out two of them before the others would be able to react. But it was too risky. They had the women inside. He wouldn't have put it past any of them to take out their gun and shoot the women in retaliation.

He observed for a few more minutes until he heard the radio on the dead man crackle.

"Come in, Pete? Where's Joe?"

He went over and turned it off. As he came out of the shed he was spotted by one of the other men. He knew the guy. His name was Leon. He was a good guy, but playing for the wrong team that night. As Leon turned to run, Jack raised his rifle and fired, hitting him in the back of the knee. He fell on the floor but not before letting off two rounds in the air.

That was the alarm.

Jack dashed towards him, shooting into his body before splitting off into a thick bush beside the house. The only advantage he had right now was darkness. It was pitch-black outside. Besides one floodlight that lit up the front area, the entire back part of the house was in darkness. The only light came from the windows. Not enough to find anyone hiding among thick evergreen bushes. Jack took a second to check his ammo. He slapped the magazine back into place.

He could hear voices. They were getting closer.

"Where is he?"

"I don't know. This is fucked up."

"I'm going back inside."

He watched them retreat into the house. They were smart. Extortion was one thing, fighting against someone hidden by darkness was foolish. They knew him. They knew his reputation for getting anyone who had double-crossed Gafino.

Jack eased up out of the bush. Three down. Maybe five or six people left. His thoughts were now with his sister and Dana. Leo wouldn't kill them. That wasn't his style. But Vito. That was something entirely different. Jack scrambled towards the door where the other two had gone. It was at the side of the house. He put his hand on the handle and tried it. It was locked. He continued around the house until he saw them through the window. One of the men had a hold of his sister by the hair. She was on her knees. A gun pointed at her head. Another went to the back door and kicked it open.

"Jack." He heard the sound of Vito's voice.

Jack stayed silent, he didn't move a muscle. His mind was reeling at the thought of losing his sister. He couldn't see Dana. He assumed they were holding her down in the basement or upstairs.

"Now you can finish this without your sister's

blood on your hands or we can do it the hard way. Do you hear me, Jack?"

Jack could see the look of fury on the man's face. Vito was bald, wearing a dark navy-blue suit. Everything about him conveyed power. The third man was scanning the windows while keeping his weapon firmly at head height.

He had no option here. They would kill her if he walked in there. They would end her life if he didn't. The Sicilians had no rule that governed women. Women were no different in their eyes. They were equally responsible for their choices and disposable.

Jack raised his assault rifle at Leo's man. The red strobe light danced on his forehead. He took a deep breath and breathed out, then pulled the trigger. The bullet tore through his head and he fell back without Milly getting hurt.

But it was a wrong choice. He watched a look of anger spread across Vito's face. Then without saying a word Vito turned. Before Jack could raise his gun, Vito fired two rounds into Milly's head. She collapsed and so did Jack. His back pressed against the wall, his mind replaying her death over and over again.

"Now, you want the other bitch to die? You come out now. Drop your weapon."

Jack wasn't paying any attention. He could barely catch his breath. They had taken the last family member left in his life. They had killed his father, they had ripped his sister from him. Now all that remained was Dana.

That was one thing he never had to worry about when he worked for Gafino. All his work was in and out. Grab, shoot, kill. There was no room for protecting others. It was what had kept him alive. He was beginning to realize what Eddie was saying. There was a choice. But you couldn't have both.

Jack got up. He loved Dana, but he couldn't think clearly. All that raced through his mind now was killing them. Instincts took over. He came towards the back of the house and began to unload round after round through the windows. Glass shattered in a deafening roar as bullets snapped. The men inside didn't have a chance to fire back as he was unleashing every single bullet he had in a sweeping fashion.

He yanked the magazine from the bottom of the rifle, tossed it and reached for another, not stopping for even a few seconds. He pressed forward as they attempted to return fire. He saw them crawling before breaking into a run and ducking back into the safety of the house. He caught one of them in the shoulder and he hit the floor screaming in pain.

What he didn't realize was that one of them had come around the side of the house. He was distracted and unable to hear the man as he was coming up behind him. He caught a glimpse of his reflection seconds before he lifted his gun. The bullet nicked his ear. A ringing sound vibrated loudly. He dropped. The man was on him faster than a tiger. They pummeled each other and rolled in the snow. The gun went off twice before he pried it loose from the man's herculean grip. Jack smashed the butt of the gun three times in the man's face.

It seemed to barely faze the guy. He rose back up, this time producing a serrated edged knife. He swept it back and forth. Jack managed to stay out of reach for a moment, but then felt his stomach burn as the man slashed him across the abdomen. Blood stained his shirt as Jack tried to wrestle the knife out of his hand.

Jack felt so much rage in that moment. He grabbed the assailant's arm, twisted and snapped it. The man screamed in agony and fell to his knees. Jack still had a hold of his limp arm behind his back. He kicked him forward onto his face. The man groaned and looked up.
"Dominick," the man yelled before Jack stepped on his back, reached down, and wrapped his forearm around his neck. He squeezed until he heard it crack. The body went limp. Jack looked up to see the barrel of a gun.

# 22

A chorus of police sirens could be heard getting closer. Dominick stared at Jack. In that moment Jack would have gladly accepted death. He was so torn up from seeing his sister brutally murdered that it no longer mattered what happened to him. He closed his eyes, waiting for the bullet to hit, but it never came. When he opened them, Dominick was gone.

Jack dragged himself to his feet. The place would be swarming with police in a matter of minutes. He heard the sound of a vehicle pulling away. He ran around to the front of the house. The SUV was gone. They were getting out before the police showed up. Jack raced over to his waiting truck, just as the police came down both ends of the road. He jumped into his truck. His heart was pounding inside his chest. His throat was burning. All he could do now was sit there as the darkness lit up with blue and red flashing lights.

Sirens blared as police approached the house. All along the road were parked vehicles. It didn't look strange that his was across the road. It blended in and likely wouldn't even be given a second glance.

As he sat and listened to police beyond his window, he curled himself as tightly as he could beneath the wheel on the floor.

It was a waiting game now.

Every few minutes he would check one of his side mirrors. His view was obstructed but as long as there were flashing lights he wasn't going anywhere. They would be looking for him. He wondered if the police had caught Vito on the way out. Hopefully, they would have Dana in custody. It was possible. Then again this wasn't their first rodeo. No doubt, they would have figured out a way to avoid the police. He wondered if they were doing the same thing as him, just further up the road. Could they have pulled in and killed the engine? Perhaps driven into someone else's driveway?

All he could think about now was, Dana. Was she alive? Had they killed her? What would he tell Jason if she was dead? He had no one else. Was Jason okay? He had to assume so. He trusted Frank.

He heard the sound of police walking back and forth. A flashlight swept across his truck. No doubt, they were performing a routine check of the area.

Hours passed until Jack fell asleep. He awoke to the sound of a motorbike starting. Its throaty exhaust pipe jolted him out of his slumber. His body was aching from being twisted into a pretzel shape under the steering wheel. A flood of memories came in, and he felt a pang of guilt. He knew he was responsible for the death of his sister. He might not have pulled the trigger, but he had forced their hand. Why didn't you get her away from there? he thought. Why didn't you put her in a treatment center on the other side of the state?

He got up and cast a glance outside. There were a couple of news vans parked outside. Some were preparing to go live. He saw several vehicles belonging to homeowners along the street pull away. No doubt, heading off to work.

Seeing police at the scene, he started the engine and pulled out behind another vehicle. Within in a matter of ten minutes, he was far away from the worst night of his life. He had one destination in mind that morning, Leo Carlone's restaurant.

When he arrived the place was closed. There were no vehicles out front. He had no idea where they could be. No sense of where to go next. For all he knew they had killed Dana and were on their way out of New York.

# 23

Frank's morning had begun like any other. He went through the numerous messages that had been left on his answering service. When he wasn't on duty, other detectives in the department dealt with any pressing matter that arose. He was unaware of what had taken place that night until he switched on the TV. He flipped through the channels until he landed on city news. A news crew was stationed outside Leo Carlone's home.

*We are at the scene of what has been called a gangland murder. Details on what took place here in the early hours of the morning are still coming in, but what we have learned so far is that there have been multiple people murdered. One of those killed was a young woman. More details will follow as we get updates.*

Frank ran a hand over his face. Oh, Jack, what have you done now? He continued poring over his messages until he got the one that Detective Harlow had left. It was to the point. *Frank, call me.* He phoned through to Harlow who was still on scene. He relayed what had happened.

"Any sign of Jack Winchester?" Frank asked.

"No, but we've found his sister. Dead."

"Shit." He paused, rubbing a hand over his face. "What about Dana Grant?"

"No sign of her but quite a number of Leo Carlone's crew are dead. One of the bodies is a guy from the hotel surveillance. Anyway, when can you get down here?"

Frank breathed out a long breath. He looked over to the sofa. Jason was asleep still.

"I'm going to need you to handle it. I will be in

later. But right now I have a few other matters to sort out."

"Sure thing."

He hung up. He needed coffee badly. Jason was beginning to stir when he went out to the kitchen. He fished around in the cupboard for a bag of coffee beans.

"Any word from Jack or my mother?" Jason asked as he rubbed sleep dust from his eyes and rolled his feet to the ground.

Frank wasn't sure how to reply to that. He didn't want to scare the kid, or send him into a blind panic. Right now they didn't know if Dana was alive or not. He couldn't cope with anyone going nuts this morning. He wasn't even used to having someone stay at his house. It was always just him. That's the way he liked it. Quiet. Peace. No one interfering in his day. Frank had grown to follow a routine every morning. He would wake up, get some coffee in him, go for a run, and do a workout. But that wasn't happening this morning.

He knew he should be more sympathetic, but when

you had worked as long as he had with the police department, you became jaded and numb. Most cops his age did. Every day he met people in dire situations. Those searching for a loved one. Those having to identify their loved one's dead body. It had at one time moved him. He would weep with people. Not anymore. He had become cold to it all. It was a means to cope. To shut out the reality of what people did to each other. It wasn't just crime families. At least with them he knew what to expect. It was the mothers who killed their toddlers, fathers who beat their children, and the pedophile rings.

The job changed you. It made you a different person. You no longer trusted anyone. You saw the world through a dark lens. It was hard to see it as being anything else than horrific.

In many ways he was sure that most officers suffered from some sort of slow PTSD. They lived with it daily. The department would encourage working out, joining a club, having some religion in your life. Anything that might take your mind off the work you had to do and the things you couldn't erase from your mind.

For Frank, his home was that. It was his personal sanctuary. And now it was being invaded with a kid that he didn't know. Damn you, Jack. Damn him for helping Frank when he was a kid. It was odd how one small event as a kid shaped his view of Jack. They had both become very different people, and yet he still believed that there was good in him. That somewhere below all the shit he had done in his life, there was that kid who wouldn't just pass by the group beating Frank. The one who came to his aid. He had to believe there was some redeeming quality left in Jack.

Truth was he had come off the tracks many times in his career. He'd been through AA meetings. Battled his own demons and been tempted to take payment from criminals in exchange for looking the other way. It was easy. He knew there were guys in the department who did exactly that. No one could prove it. It was always kept hush-hush, but it was common knowledge.

Jason wandered out to the kitchen as Frank ground

up coffee beans, shook the grains into a French press, and poured hot water over it. The smell brought his senses to life. Kick-starting his mind to think more clearly.

"I haven't heard anything about them. You want some breakfast?"

"Sure," Jason replied.

"What do you want? I've got toast, cereal."

"Whatever you're having."

"I don't eat breakfast. Just coffee," Frank said.

"What's the cereal for?"

"The evening," Frank said.

"You mean you only eat cereal in the evening?"

"Late at night, if I get hungry."

"But not in the morning?"

"No. Coffee suits me fine. I'm lucky if I have ten minutes to myself. I'm usually racing out the door."

"Doesn't sound like much of a life."

"It isn't. Don't become a cop, kid."

"I have no plans on it."

"Coffee?"

Jason nodded.

He poured him a cup and slid it across. They sat there in silence drinking coffee. Frank made Jason some toast. Half an hour had passed when Jack came stumbling into the room. His face was pale, and it wasn't immediately obvious that he was hurt until he pulled his hand out and it was covered in dried blood.

"Jack." Jason jumped up and gave him a hand over to the sofa.

"Oh my God, Jack. What have you done now?"

Jack looked up at Frank. Frank went and got a towel, a bowl of water, a small first-aid kit, and some bandages.

"They killed her, Frank."

"I heard about. It's all over the news," he replied.

Frank tore open Jack's shirt and began tending to the wound.

"What happened?" Frank asked.

Frank went about cleaning up the wound while Jack brought him up to speed. By the time he was done, a pile of bloody rags was on the counter. The water had turned a deep red.

"Did you see where they went?" Frank asked.

"They drove off."

"How the hell did you get into all of this, Jack?"

"Long story."

The following hour, Frank listened to Jack as he told him what had occurred with Gafino. He shared with him what happened after getting out of Rikers. And how he had planned to leave it all behind.

"So what now?" Frank asked.

"I have to find them, they have Dana."

Jason dropped his head into his hands.

"You think you know where they might have gone?"

"I went by Leo's place but it was closed. They could be anywhere by now. I need your help," Jack said.

"I can't help you. Hell, I should be bringing you in."

"I understand," Jack replied.

"Just give me a moment."

"You going to call it in?"

"No."

Frank left the room and went upstairs. He took a shower and put on some fresh clothes. When he was faced with challenges, he always found a shower worked wonders. There must have been something about the water hitting the head, or the steam clearing his mind but it did the job.

He sat there on this bed and glanced at a photo of his ex. He still hadn't removed it. He hadn't even slept in this room since they had parted ways. Most nights he would just fall asleep in the La-Z-Boy downstairs. Now here he was thinking about what he should do. He had already put in twenty years of service. He'd joined the police when he was nineteen. He'd always had his eyes fixed on promotion. Becoming the chief. Laying down the rules and helping the police department become the best. So much had changed in that time. The longer he was in the force, the more jaded he had become. He no longer wanted the responsibility that came with being a chief, or any position for that matter, besides the one he had. The higher up you went, the more shit you had to deal with. Everyone blamed the one at the top.

He glanced at his phone. He thought about calling it in and having them arrive without sirens blaring so they could take Jack into custody. Regardless of them finding the others, Jack had done enough to put him away for life. He was certain of that. How they would prove it, was another thing entirely.

On the other hand, he could use this as a way to put a mighty big dent in the activities of the crime syndicate. He could finish out his career a hero. The guy who brought down the New York and Sicilian Mafia. It had a nice ring to it. He could see it now in the news. Veteran cop makes good on his promise. He'd made that promise years ago. As a naïve young detective. In a time when he thought he could change things. Long before he realized how difficult it was to catch crime families. He had been trying to do it for years. But there was only so much he had been able to achieve. He had needed someone on the inside. Someone who knew how they operated. Or someone who the Mafia wanted dead. Jack was the perfect person for this. It made sense. Help him, to help himself. Kill two birds with one stone and repay him for what he did when they were younger.

# 24

The phone call came in while Frank was upstairs. Vito had made the call. Dana was still alive. They briefly had placed her on the phone.

When they did, she was crying.

Jack didn't tell Jason, but he had a feeling he already knew. As much as Jack wanted to trust Frank, he knew he couldn't. It wasn't that he didn't think he would help him. But they were fighting two different wars.

He had no intentions of letting any of them live. Whereas Frank would have done everything by the book. Trouble was these were the kind of men that could operate even from within a maximum-security prison. Their reach extended far beyond the thick walls and barbed wire.

He had figured that others would come. Vincent told him that. He knew that. That's what he would have done had Gafino still been alive. There had been times Jack had wondered what life would have been like had he just gone back to being a debt collector for the mob. He never lingered long on that thought as he knew where that road ended.

Vito wanted to meet in the Annadale neighborhood of Staten Island. He'd said that the death of his sister was payback for the money they had lost and the death of Leo's son. In his mind they were even. Now he wanted to talk about a truce. Having Jack come work for him. He could use a man of his skillset. As if that was ever going to happen. Did he really think Jack was that stupid?

He would kill him the first chance he got. If reputation meant a lot to Gafino, it was everything to the Sicilian Mafia. And what better way to regain control than to kill a man who was infamous in New York? It would send out a clear message. That no one was to fuck with them or they would wind up dead.

At first it puzzled him as to why they would want to meet there. Then it dawned on him. Gafino had a waterfront property. It was nestled in the Blue Heron Park Preserve. The entire place was surrounded by marshes, fishing ponds, and hiking trails. It was a four-million-dollar house that overlooked Raritan Bay.

Jack had left before Frank had returned. He had tried to get Jason to stay, but he wouldn't. He said if his mother died and he was just sitting around he wouldn't be able to live with himself. Reluctantly Jack took him along. Even at the age of sixteen, Jason reminded him of himself. The thought that he could get hurt was far from his mind. Though he knew it was a possibility. He would deal with that later.

As they drove away from Frank's place, Jack winced in pain. The cut wasn't deep. But damn, it hurt like shit.

There were several ways to get over to Staten Island: The most common was by ferry. It transported over twenty-two million passengers across the water every year.

It ran twenty-four hours and took around five minutes to get you from lower Manhattan to Bay Street on the island. The other ways were to go by vehicle across the Verrazano-Narrows Bridge from Brooklyn or take one of the bridges from New Jersey.

They were taking the truck, so it was over the bridge they went.

That morning there was a clear blue sky. It gave them a spectacular view of the New York skyline and the Statue of Liberty. Before they went, Jack stopped at the storage locker, stocked up on ammo, and retrieved a second assault rifle. He snatched up a bulletproof vest. He paused at the door and spotted the case of grenades. It was extreme, but then so was this situation.

"I want to go with you."

"It's too dangerous."

"What will happen after?" Jason asked.

"What?"

"You know, if everything goes right. Will you return with us?"

He floored the gas pedal as they tore out of the storage area.

"Right now, Jason, nothing matters except getting your mother back."

The journey over there was long and slow because of all the traffic.

"I'm sorry about your sister," Jason said.

The car idled on the bridge. Jack looked out over the water. He didn't respond. He was lost in thought. His mind drifted back to when they were kids. To a time when things felt good. Those moments were few, so they stuck out in his mind. He remembered taking his sister out. Going to Staten Island for the first time. They rode the ferry over there. They were meant to be at school that day but he'd convinced her not to go. When they weren't in school, they were usually dealing with shit at home. It ate away at them. It was breaking down his sister. He could see the way the light was dimming in her eyes. The way she lost a sense of confidence and hope for life. He just wanted one day. One day when they had nobody yelling at them. No one hitting them. No one telling them what to do.

It had been a Wednesday. They never got on the school bus that day. Jack was fifteen at the time, she was almost ten. When they reached the other side of the island, they spent the whole day exploring. They bought ice cream and hung out in some creepy old mental hospital that used to be operational. It was called Willowbrook State School. Geraldo Rivera had run a piece on it, exposing the horrors that had occurred there. Children sat in their own feces, kids were beaten by staff, and there was a lot of sexual abuse that had gone on. The place was closed in 1987.

After exploring what remained of a gutted building, they found it a little too creepy and left.

From there they had spent a few hours fishing and bathing in the sunshine. They daydreamed and talked about what life would be like if they had been born into a wealthy family.

As Jack came back into the present moment he

switched into high gear. He knew there would likely be more than just a few men there this time. Leo would have pulled in more help from surrounding crime families. Those they were still associated with were few. Everything had dwindled in the city. The grip they once had over businesses was starting to lose its power. The police had cracked down on numerous areas that were being extorted and put away a number of key figures.

Their time was nearly over. And he planned on being the one who put the final nail in the coffin.

"This Danny guy, how does he operate?" Jack asked.

Jason tossed him a glance. "Uh." He paused, contemplating the question. "He stores some drugs at a place outside of Rockland Cove, distributes them out of the condo in town, and receives shipments each month on a boat called the Morning Glory."

"Down at the harbor?"

"Yeah. That's where he keeps any of the overflow. They keep it stashed under the seats on the boat."

"What will you do when you go back?" Jack asked.

"Well, besides wanting to kill the guy?"

"Jason."

"I'm kidding. I'm gonna stay clear of it all."

"That might not work so well," Jack replied.

"Maybe I will tip off the police."

"Maybe somebody already has?"

"No. He is very sneaky. Somehow he knows when the police patrol. He has scanners and shit."

"Then they need to show up when he's not awake."

"Yeah. I would love to see his face when that day happens."

As Jack came closer to the location, he pulled into Blue Heron Park Preserve. It was a tourist location that had been acquired by the city. It was a wildlife sanctuary that had been built upon a wasteland of abandoned cars. Now it was picturesque in more ways than one. Full of walking trails, meadows, ponds, streams, and woodlands. It offered the best cover.

Jack knew that it was a good hike through the

marshlands to get to the home. Thankfully the trails would keep him dry. Jack killed the engine.

"Now remember. If I'm not back in thirty minutes, you are to phone Frank, let him know what happened. He'll take it from there. Here's a phone." He gave him the card with Frank's number on it.

"I'm not waiting here. I can help."

"You're too young, Jason. We're not doing this now."

"But."

"No. Enough," Jack bellowed.

Jason looked taken aback.

"Now remember. Thirty minutes."

Jack jumped out, reached into the back of the truck, and put on the bulletproof vest. Over the top of that he put on a belt that would hold the magazines. By the time he was finished getting geared up, he was starting to resemble a special ops guy. He had enough weapons and ammo to cause some serious damage. He took extra in a duffel bag, just in case. He would leave it close to the house. In the event things went south, he would have a backup option.

He gave Jason one final glance and then trudged his way down a trail until the truck was out of sight.

* * *

Jason sat there for a moment weighing his options. There was no way one man could pull this off. He stared at the card before tapping it against his leg. Jack's sister had already died. He wasn't going to let the same thing happen to his mother.

Jason made the call to Frank.

"Frank?"

"Where are you, Jason?"

"Staten Island."

He relayed the information of where he was and what Jack was up to. Frank told him to stay put. He would be there within the next fifteen minutes

Fifteen? It had taken them the better part of an hour to get out here because of traffic. He assumed they were going to take a helicopter.

* * *

Dana fully expected that she was going to die. She had heard the gunfire, she had seen that Milly hadn't returned. Though no one had told her that she was dead, she just figured she was. Now, all she could think about was her boy. It had been a huge mistake opening herself back up to Jack. Trusting him to keep her out of harm's way.

After leaving Long Island, Vito had been furious. Dominick had wanted to return to kill Jack but Leo had told them it was too risky. The police were in the area. She heard police drive by their parked vehicle. She was on the floor of the SUV. How close she was to being found. Now she had no idea where she was. She had heard them say on numerous occasions that it was best if they just killed her and dumped her body. Vito was keen to get out of New York. He wanted to cut ties with Leo. She heard everything. For the longest part of the journey out to wherever they were now, they had been arguing about what to do.

She had heard the ocean and seen it briefly when they took her into a mansion. It was massive. They took her into a back room and one of Leo's men was watching over her. He'd been given instructions that if she did anything to try to escape, he was to shoot her. She sat on a sofa, her hands tied behind her back, while the guy glared at her from the opposite side of the room. She could tell he was undressing her with his eyes. He would smirk occasionally. There was no indication of time. No clocks on the walls.

"You think you could loosen these binds?"

"Nope."

"But they are cutting into my skin."

The guy glanced at the door. He walked over and stood in front of her.

"What will you do for me?"

"Forget it. I would rather be in pain."

He chuckled and walked back to his spot.

* * *

Jack had eyes on the place. He had brought a small

pair of military binoculars with him. He was trying to gauge how many men there were. He wasn't going to take chances like he did last time. It had got his sister killed. He needed to act swiftly this time. There were six men patrolling the house. He saw another through a window. Leo and Vito were out of sight. He knew now they wouldn't hesitate to kill her. For all he knew, they could have killed her by now.

He was ready to engage and move in on the house when he heard the helicopter. It was subtle at first, then shots rang out. He glanced up to see it. The word POLICE was on the side in a deep blue.

He chuckled. Jason.

It was now or never. He attached the suppressor on the end of the weapon. He pushed ahead. One of the men was distracted by the helicopter when Jack fired two rounds into him. He dropped and Jack unleashed two more into the guy who came rushing around the corner. Jack dived for cover and waited.

Police were closing in on them. It would keep the

guys on the outside busy while he ducked inside and began searching for Dana.

He pulled at a door and entered into a pool area.

* * *

Frank did what was expected of him under the circumstances. He notified the rest of his team that he had just got a lead. Sicilian Mafia were out at a Staten Island residence, heavily armed and preparing to attack another crime family. It was partly true. He gave them just enough for them to take it seriously. SWAT had been notified and two helicopters had been dispatched. He was on one, SWAT was on another. Local Staten Island police had been notified and were en route as well. One car had been dispatched to pick up Jason.

* * *

Jack could hear the sound of the two helicopters as he walked slowly around the pool area. It was humid inside like stepping into a hot sauna. Sweat dripped down his back. He was coming around the side of the pool when one of Leo's men appeared off to his right side. He went by the name Joey Dee. Both of them knew each other. They had worked together seven or eight years ago. He was one of Leo's right-hand men. Lethal with his hands but shit at shooting. Both of them unloaded their guns at each other. The walls were peppered and glass shattered.

"Ah, come on, Jack. Let's talk this out," Joey said.

Jack crouched, hiding behind an overturned table. He lifted his gun over and used the window's reflection to fire in the right direction. He had to hope that at least one bullet would hit him. None of them did.

"You know they think you are legend around these parts? But I know better than that. You're just another kid with a chip on his shoulder."

Another round was fired, followed by one more.

"One hell of a fighter, they say. So how about it? You, me? No weapons."

Jack paused firing for a moment. They were all the same. It was a pride thing. Always trying to one up each other in crime families. Test each other to see what the other was made of. No one wanted to think they were less than another.

"Sure," Jack replied.

He peeked out and saw Joey lay down his gun and slowly appear from behind a wall. Jack lifted his gun to show him that he was going to place it on the ground. Joey was on the other side of the pool. Slowly Jack made his way out behind the table and lowered the assault rifle. Both men were careful. They didn't take their eyes off each other.

"I think I'll make that woman of yours mine after this," Joey said, smirking.

"Keep on talking shit," Jack replied.

"You know this can only end one way for you, Jack. You are outnumbered and let's face it. I always was a better fighter."

They began making their way around the pool toward each other. He was within a few feet when Jack instantly reached around his back, pulled out his Glock in one smooth motion, and fired a round into his skull.

Joey dropped into the pool.

“Fighting is overrated,” Jack said.

# 25

Leo Carlone hated Vito Nicchi. After Long Island he wanted to call it off. He loved his son but what was done, was done. They had taken the life of Jack's sister. That was revenge enough. Not that he would have done it. Vito had signed his own death sentence by pulling that trigger. Leo wanted Jack dead and would have gone to great lengths and risk in those first few months after hearing about his son's death. But after a year, it became less personal and more about covering ass with the Sicilian Mafia.

Vito wouldn't back down. He didn't just want payment for the loss; he wanted a large chunk of the New York drug business, and to ensure that business continued as usual. But Leo wasn't into the drug business. It wasn't his thing. Gafino had handled that. He merely offered his support as did the other older members of the Mafia. All he wanted in his old age was to run his restaurant and lounge and retire in a year or two.

That wasn't going to happen now. He heard the sound of helicopters outside. One came into view and he squeezed his eyes shut trying to calm his nerves.

If they had just let it go, but they wouldn't. He wouldn't, to be specific. They had cheated the police once and got away, but there was no chance that was going to happen again. The place was surrounded, helicopters would spot them coming out. Fuck! he thought.

He'd considered shooting Vito himself. At least that way when Jack showed up he could try to convince him that he was forced into it and had taken matters into his hands to right the wrong. But Vito scared him. It seemed odd to think that anyone could make him feel fear. He had spent his youth rising through the ranks of the Mafia. He had killed and made grown men cry. But

Vito was a whole different kettle of fish.

"We need to get out of here," Leo said.

"We aren't going anywhere until he's dead," Vito replied.

Leo gave a wave of his hand. "Forget him."

"He killed one of my men."

"And you killed his sister. I think we're even."

He stepped closer, making Leo swallow hard. "I'll decide that."

"I think we have bigger matters to deal with," Dominick said, gesturing outside to the SWAT officers who were now on the ground.

Vito paced up and down. Leo could see he was losing control of the situation. In a matter of minutes Jack would be here, and if not him, SWAT would burst in with flash grenades dropping and bullets flying. Then it wouldn't matter.

Leo didn't want to go back to prison. He had done his time fourteen years ago. It had been a long stretch for extortion. He vowed never to get involved in anything that would jeopardize his family. And here he was, breaking that promise.

* * *

Dana knew she had seen him before. The local news had run a piece on the Sicilian Mafia three years ago. Twenty of their men had been arrested in New York after the feds seized a large shipment of heroin that had been brought into the New York harbor. At that time Vito Nicchi had received a lot of press about his ties with leading crime families in New Jersey.

Back then, Matt was alive. He'd been reading the piece with great interest. She didn't realize his interest was because he was involved with distribution of drugs to the New York Mafia.

Now, she sat on a marble floor watched by several thugs with Glocks. There was nothing for her to do but think about everything that had led up to this moment. Where was her son? What she would do if she ever got out of this? What would happen if she were killed? She had considered how much Jack meant to her and weighed it against a life without him. Maybe it was because she had been through so much with Matt that she couldn't cope with it well. She loved Jack, and there was a good chance they could have had a life together. But it would always be eating away at the back of her mind. The what-ifs. What if the Mafia showed up again? What if her son was murdered? What if Jack turned on her? He said he wouldn't touch her but how could she know? They all seemed like savages. Men driven by power, greed, and a lust for blood.

* * *

"Dominick, take a few of the men and post them around the main entrances. I don't want any surprises. Anyone comes in, kill them."

Dominick nodded, gestured to six of the men and they followed him. Vito had been in these situations. He was stressed, but he knew the police wouldn't come in without a plan. They had no idea how many were in here, or if they had hostages. There were too many variables. They hadn't even attempted to phone in. Unless they fired at the cops, they wouldn't send in SWAT. The police had more sense than that. They had to assess the situation.

Vito walked over to a decanter of bourbon and poured himself a glass. He let it slip back. Its warmth took the edge off what he was feeling. He glanced at Dana. She was just a pawn in his game. Had the police not shown up, he had considered taking her with him. She had a good body on her. He could put her to good use.

# 26

Both helicopters landed beyond the mansion. Frank jumped out and met with several officers who had already arrived on scene. In that moment, there was no gunfire to be heard. However, the media would be all over this within the hour. The place would then be swarming with news channel helicopters and press trying to get through.

"I need you to set up a roadblock on the east and west side. No one gets in or out, especially the media. The last thing I want is them screwing this up," Frank said.

"Got it."

An officer ran towards his cruiser. Frank was behind a cruiser when one of the SWAT officers came over.

"What have we got here?"

"Multiple assailants. Are you going in?" Frank asked.

"We need to assess the situation further before we move in."

"If you don't get in there fast, you are going to have a bloodbath on your hands."

"You mentioned knowing one of them. Is he a threat?"

Frank hadn't mentioned Jack's name. Only that he knew two of the people inside. He was about to answer when his phone rang.

"Sir, we've arrived on scene but there is no kid here."

"What?"

"The truck is empty."

"Shit."

* * *

Jason was damn sure he wasn't going to wait

around for police. After placing the call to Frank he'd hopped out of the truck and followed the same path that Jack had taken. He knew it was dangerous, foolish even. But the thought of waiting on the sidelines wasn't going to happen. Jason pushed his way through the thick reeds that were covered in snow. He followed the footprints that led up to the huge mansion. He could hear the sound of a chopper overhead. He had no clue what he was going to do. Jack had taken the guns.

* * *

Jack had made his way into the heart of the house. He could hear Leo and Vito arguing. Then he saw them. He kept close to the wall. Leo was blaming Vito for the way he had handled this. Shouting and waving his hand in his face. Vito was threatening Leo. Telling him to mind his tongue or he would silence him.

"You think he's going to show up here with all the police? You are out of your mind," Leo said.

"He'll show." Vito was unconvinced by Leo's words.

"You don't know him like I do," Leo replied.

"It doesn't matter now. This is over. I'm out of here," Leo added.

Vito pulled his gun. "You are not going anywhere. You still owe me money. Besides, police are everywhere."

Jack had ducked his head out to see where Dana was when Dominick spotted him. Dominick unloaded round after round at the wall. Jack ran for cover. Pieces of concrete flew in the air, cutting Jack's face. He was using a submachine gun. He didn't let up. He was getting closer. Jack pulled his assault rifle around and returned fire. The place was covered in a fine dust as bullets peppered the walls.

"Jack," he heard the sound of Vito's voice. "Come on out or I swear I will end her life right now."

* * *

Officers outside were now ducking behind their cars. Several of them had fired off rounds. The sound of gunfire was all they needed to hear; the SWAT team were ready to go. Fully kitted out in their gear, they were lined up checking their weapons. They just needed the go-ahead.

"Hold your fire," an officer yelled.

"You are going to have to go in there," Frank said.

The officer in charge nodded and indicated to his men to move in.

* * *

Meanwhile Jason had made his way into the house through the same door that led into the pool area. He saw the body in the pool. The water had turned a deep red. His pulse was racing hard. He spotted a handgun on the floor. He scooped it up and continued on.

* * *

Jack wasn't going to risk Dana's life. He knew Vito would kill her, yet he also knew the moment he put down his weapon and came out, Vito would kill them both. He pressed his back against a wall and banged his head several times trying to think.

"Come on. Don't make me wait."

Against his better judgment Jack came out. He

didn't immediately throw down his gun. He kept it focused on them as he walked closer.

"Put it down," Dominick yelled.

As he was approaching them he saw Leo try to dart out of the room. Vito didn't hesitate, he turned and fired off a round. Leo hit the ground. A pool of blood began to form around his head.

"Fucking guy just wouldn't listen," Vito said.

Jack's eyes widened.

"Look. Let her go. She has nothing to do with this."

"Oh but she does," Vito said.

"Put the gun down, Jack," Dominick told him.

"What, so you can kill me?"

He kept his eyes firmly fixed on Dominick.

"You've got me all wrong, Jack. You've cost me millions of dollars. Destroyed our association with New York. So you're going to pay me back. You're coming with us back to Italy. You'll work with Dominick. We've heard of your reputation. You'll be a great asset to the team."

"What?" Dominick turned around, shocked by what he was hearing from his boss.

"He's no use to us dead. But his skillset. We can use that. Simple as that. You come work for us. I'll let her go right now."

"You expect me to believe that?"

"I don't expect you to believe anything. But weigh your options. I can kill you both now and walk away, or you can put in some time and work for me."

Jack assessed the situation. There were four of Leo Carlone's men pointing guns at him, as well as Dominick. Vito had the muzzle of his gun pressed against Dana's head. She was crying uncontrollably. She didn't stand a chance here.

"Fine."

"Good?" Vito asked for confirmation.

Jack nodded.

"Put the gun down then," Vito said again.

"Let her go first."

"You really aren't in a position to be negotiating here."

He knew Vito was lying. There was no way in hell he was going to all this trouble to have Jack work for him. It was a ploy. He also didn't want to just kill him. Otherwise Leo's men would have fired by now. No, he wanted to inflict real pain.

Jack swallowed hard. He had no intention of giving up his weapon but he began lowering it. As he got closer to the floor, the sound of glass shattering was followed by Vito holding his chest. He turned his hand over. It was covered in blood. He glanced at Jack, then fell to the floor dead. SWAT had taken him out.

"Run," Jack yelled at Dana. Dana was up and scrambling towards another room when Dominick turned the gun on her. Jack hadn't fully lowered his gun when he squeezed the trigger. The bullet from Jack's gun hit Dominick in the leg, knocking his legs out from beneath him. He fell to the floor and then bullets began to snap in every direction. SWAT were moving in. Leo Carlone's men began engaging with them and holding them back with submachine guns.

It was pure chaos.

Dominick was already up and hobbling in the direction of Dana. He unleashed a flurry of rounds at Jack. Jack couldn't get across the room without being hit by bullets. He watched as one of Leo's men fell to the floor. In a matter of minutes this place would be swarming with cops. But that was the least of his concerns right now. He had to get to Dana before Dominick.

Jack took out one of Leo's men as he dashed across the room under a hail of bullets. Furniture, glass, slices of concrete were going everywhere. A cloud of concrete dust made it hard to see.

Jack slid across the floor on both knees while shooting.

He had managed to get over to the other side partially unscathed with only one hit in the arm. Jack had felt the searing burn of a bullet before. He was in pain but could still move. As he stumbled into the room that both

Dana and Dominick had disappeared into, he found himself staring at Jason. Jason had a gun raised at Dominick. Dana was on the floor with Dominick pointing his weapon at her.

"I will kill her right now." He paused. "Put your gun down," Dominick said.

"Dominick, it's over."

"No, she's my way out of here."

Jack had his gun leveled at Dominick's head. There was a fifty-fifty chance that if he shot him, his reflexes wouldn't cause his own gun to go off.

"Jason, put the gun down," Jack said.

"No," he replied.

"Jason, you don't want to do this. There's no going back once you've taken a life. Don't do this."

Jason's hand was shaking. Their eyes darted between one another. Finally, he began lowering the gun. As he did, Dominick turned his gun towards Jason. Before he had it leveled, Jack blasted two rounds into Dominick's skull. He collapsed in a heap.

Jason ran over to Dana.

"Jason." Dana wrapped her arms around him. Tears were flowing. Jack turned and saw SWAT had taken out Leo's men. He discarded his weapon, and everything that made it look as though he was anything more than a victim. He huddled together with Dana and Jason.

All he could say was, "I'm so sorry."

SWAT burst into the room clearing each one.

"We've got three in here."

They waited there for a few minutes until Frank appeared. He glanced at Jack and shook his head.

"You guys hurt?" Frank asked

"Just me," Jack muttered.

Frank turned and shouted, "Get a medic in here."

Everything played out slowly over the next half an hour. Jack watched as SWAT and medics roamed through the house searching for victims and other potential threats. As he was led out to an ambulance, the home looked like a war zone. Jason and Dana sat huddled together casting glances over to Jack.

He knew it was over.

That this would be the last time he would see them. He fully expected to find himself locked away in a maximum-security prison for the rest of his life. An ambulance rushed him away to hospital. The police escorted Dana and Jason away in a cruiser.

# 27

When Jack arrived at North Shore Staten Island Hospital, it didn't take them long to attend to his wound and pull the bullet out of his arm. He had been there for several hours before Frank showed up. When he appeared, Jack thought he had a sense of what he was going to say. He was completely wrong.

Frank came in with two cups of coffee. He placed one on the bedside table and took a seat. Without saying a word, he sat there for a while sipping his.

"Here to arrest me, Frank?"

"I haven't decided yet."

Jack gave him a confused look.

"Dana confirmed what you told me about trying to

get out of it all."

"Try," he paused, "would be the appropriate word."

"With Gafino, Leo, and the head of the Sicilian Mafia gone, that should be a lot easier for you, right?"

"Well, that depends on what you plan to do?"

Frank breathed in deeply and took another drink from his cup.

"Amazing to think how far we've come, isn't it? Two kids from New Jersey wind up on the opposite side of the tracks. I've put away more criminals than most of the guys in the department. You've killed more people than most of the mob combined. It could easily have been me in your shoes."

Jack listened, nodding slowly.

"I'm sorry about your sister and Eddie. Eddie was a good man."

"He was my father."

Frank glanced at him intently. "For real?"

Jack nodded.

"Then, I'm really sorry."

Jack took a sip of his drink. It was hot. He placed it back on the table.

"Is Dana and Jason still in New York?"

"No, they've returned home."

"Did they say anything to you about me that I should know?"

Frank smiled. "No. I think you know that ship has sailed, Jack."

They sat there for five minutes drinking their coffee. Like two old friends who were comfortable in each other's presence. Once Frank was done, he tossed the Styrofoam cup into the garbage.

"Well. It's been good seeing you again, Jack."

Frank straightened up and walked to the door. Jack was stunned. Frank paused there and turned back.

"Oh, your truck," he tossed Jack the keys. "I had it brought up around back."

"Thanks. What are you going to tell them?" Jack asked.

"Nothing to say. You were held hostage. No one

saw you kill anyone."

He studied Frank's face.

"But I ran from that security guard."

"Fear," Frank replied.

Jack tipped his head to one side.

"Oh, I think the infamous Jack Winchester gets scared once in a while."

The corner of Frank's lip curled up.

"Just promise me one thing," Frank said.

"Sure."

"You won't return to New York."

Jack let out a stifled laugh. Frank smiled and then left.

* * *

Over the course of the following days, Jack thought a lot about his time in New York while healing up in that hospital. He should have stayed longer. They wanted him to stay for a week or so, but Jack wasn't going to take any more chances. As much as he was convinced that it was over, and that the threat to him was gone, he didn't want to linger around to find out. Within four days he had checked out.

Outside he found his truck exactly where Frank had said it would be. He returned to the storage unit and filled the cab with everything that Eddie had left behind. It wasn't much.

He wasn't entirely sure why Frank let him go. He could have pulled him in on numerous charges. But perhaps it was his way of repaying what Jack had done for him years ago. Frank understood what it meant to be surrounded by a crowd that only wanted to see you bleed. Maybe he wanted to be the one that came along and stopped a fight. Or perhaps he understood that the line between good and bad was nothing more than a decision. A decision that either could help someone or destroy them. Had Jack not stepped in that day on the streets of New Jersey, maybe Frank might not have let him go. Or maybe it was just part of the path they were meant to take. The lesson they were meant to learn.

Either way he was grateful for a chance to get out.

Where the road would take him was anyone's guess. He stood beside his truck and tried phoning Dana's cell. It came back as out of service. He rang the landline of their home. It returned the same message. Whatever road they had taken, it would be without him. He loved her and he could have found her, but the best thing he could do for her was to stay far away. To keep his distance and allow Dana and Jason a chance at a life without the baggage that he brought to the table. Maybe one day she would find someone who could see her the way he saw her. A guy who would treat her the way he loved her.

He made one final phone call.

It was anonymous, to the Rockland Cove police. He gave them information about Danny Regan's drug setup three miles outside of Rockland Cove. He told them how Danny was receiving shipments. He instructed them to check out the seats on the boat called Morning Glory. He also suggested they didn't radio any of this information out and to hit the place early in the morning. They wanted Jack's name, but he hung up. He tossed his phone on the floor and crunched it beneath his boot.

He smiled at the thought of Danny having his door kicked in sometime in the early hours of the morning. Everyone had to learn the hard way. Danny Regan was no different. His time had run out. Perhaps if there was a next time, he would listen.

Jason had said he would like to be there to see Danny's face. It would have been sweet but not as satisfying as seeing Jason's the day he would learn about Danny's fate. He felt a twinge of disappointment in his gut. The thought that he wouldn't be around to watch him grow. To see the man that he would become. But more than anything to finish his days beside Dana. Nevertheless, he knew staying away was the best thing for all of them.

Change was on the horizon.

The very last item he was about to place into the truck was a laptop. It was partially charged when he opened it. He sat for a moment on the upside-down bucket and browsed through the folders on the desktop.

He searched the offline emails, and that's when he began to see a clearer picture form of what Eddie had done for a living.

People hired him to fix problems. But these weren't the typical problems. They were ones that most wouldn't be able to fix. The ones that got overlooked by a flawed legal system. They fell into the gray areas. They were jobs that brought a silent war to an enemy that often remained unseen. The kind of people he used to work for.

He had a chance to right his wrongs. To use his skills for good. To follow in the footsteps of his father. Somewhere he hoped Eddie was looking down on him. Grinning.

There was much he would still have to learn. But he had time now.

Jack brought the steel door down on the now empty storage unit. He locked it and returned the key to the main office. He informed them that it would no longer be needed and then returned to his vehicle.

Jack hopped into the truck. He adjusted his mirrors,

turned on his GPS. He pulled out the photo he had taken from Eddie's. The one that was inside the Bible. He glanced at the name, John Dalton. The address was for a place in Los Angeles. He tapped it into the GPS, gave a quick glance in his mirror, cranked the radio up, and pulled away.

* * *

THANK YOU FOR READING

Debt Collector: Vengeance Book #2

Debt Collector 3: Reborn is Available

# NEWSLETTER

Thank you for buying Debt Collector 2:Vengeance.

Building a relationship with readers is one of the best things about writing. I occasionally send out a newsletter with details on new releases and subscriber only special offers. For instance, with each new release of a book, you will be alerted to it at a subscriber only discounted rate. No one else will be alerted to that price. Which means you can get your hands on it for around 80% off. But it's only available for 24hrs at that price and it's only offered to subscribers. Not even those following on social media will know about that deal. Also you will be privy to FREE books as I make them available.

Go here to receive special offers, bonus content, and news about Jon's new books, sign up for the newsletter. http://www.jonmills.com/

# A PLEA...

If you enjoyed the book, I would really appreciate it if you would consider leaving a review. I can't stress how helpful this is in helping other readers decide if they should give it a shot. Reviews from readers like you are the best recommendation a book can have. Without reviews, an author's books are virtually invisible on the retail sites. It also lets me know what you liked. You can leave a review by visiting the book's page. I would greatly appreciate it. It only takes a couple of seconds.

Thank you — **Jon Mills**

# JON MILLS

Jon Mills is originally from England. He currently lives in Ontario, Canada with his family. He is the author of The Debt Collector, The Promise and the Undisclosed Trilogy. To get more information about upcoming books or if you wish to get in touch with Jon, you can do so using the following contact information:

Twitter: Jon_Mills

Facebook: /authorjonmills

Website: www.jonmills.com

Email: contact@jonmills.com

Made in the USA
San Bernardino, CA
23 May 2018